7/10

LP
FICTION   Goldenbaum, Sally.
Gol

A murder of taste

DUE DATE   MCN   07/10   32.95

A Murder of Taste

Center Point
Large Print

Also by Sally Goldenbaum
and available from Center Point Large Print:

Death by Cashmere

The Queen Bees Quilt Mystery Series
Murders on Elderberry Road

A Murder of Taste

A Queen Bees Quilt Mystery

Sally Goldenbaum

CENTER POINT PUBLISHING
THORNDIKE, MAINE

This Center Point Large Print edition
is published in the year 2010 by arrangement with
Kansas City Star Books.

Cover illustration: Neil Nakahodo
Character illustrations: Lon Eric Craven

The text of this Large Print edition is unabridged.
In other aspects, this book may vary
from the original edition.
Printed in the United States of America
on permanent paper.
Set in 16-point Times New Roman type.

ISBN: 978-1-60285-823-7

Library of Congress Cataloging-in-Publication Data

Goldenbaum, Sally.
  A murder of taste : a queen bees quilt mystery / Sally Goldenbaum. — Center Point
large print ed.
    p. cm.
  Originally published: Kansas City, MO : Kansas City Star Books, © 2004.
  ISBN 978-1-60285-823-7 (library binding : alk. paper)
  1. Quiltmakers—Fiction. 2. Large type books. I. Title.
PS3557.O35937M86 2010
813′.54—dc22
                                                                    2010009465

CAST OF CHARACTERS

PORTIA (PO) PALTROW, founder and nurturer of the Queen Bees quilting group. Anchors the women's quilting group in life and in art.

KATE SIMPSON, Po's goddaughter and a graduate student at the college. The newest member of the Queen Bees.

PHOEBE MELLON, wife to Jimmy, an up-and-coming lawyer, young mother to two-year-old twins, and a constant surprise to her quilting cohorts.

ELEANOR CANTERBURY,
who lives on the edge of the
college her great-grandfather
founded. Is heir to the
Canterbury family fortune.

LEAH SARANDON,
professor of women's studies
at Canterbury College. An
artistic quilter.

SELMA PARKER,
owner of Parker's Dry Goods
Store. Provides a weekly
gathering place for the Queen
Bees quilting group and
generous doses of
down-home wisdom.

SUSAN MILLER,
Selma's artistic assistant manager in the quilt shop. Recently returned to college to pursue a degree in fiber arts.

MAGGIE HELMERS,
Crestwood's favorite veterinarian. Is an avid quilter and collector of fat lady art.

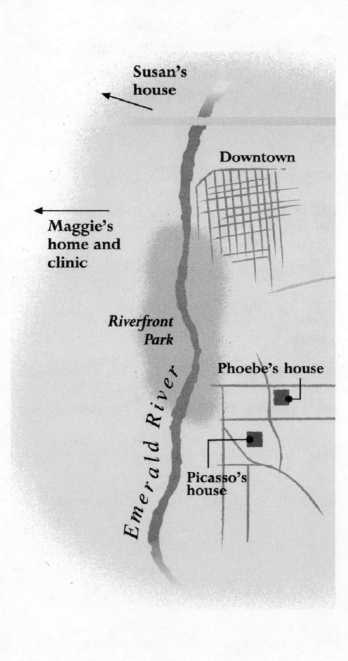

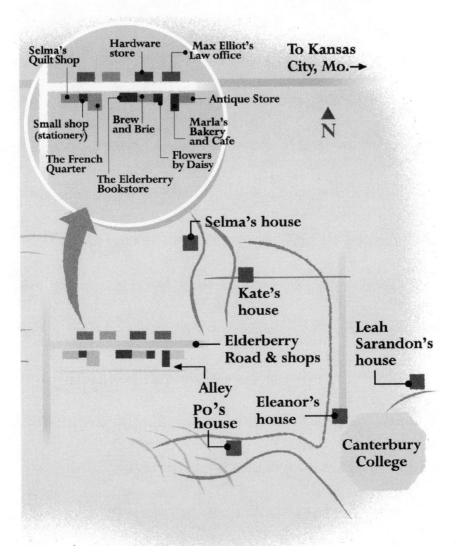

Selma's
Quilt Shop

Hardware
store

Max Elliot's
Law office

To Kansas
City, Mo. →

Antique Store

N

Small shop
(stationery)

Brew
and Brie

Marla's
Bakery
and Cafe

The French
Quarter

Flowers
by Daisy

The Elderberry
Bookstore

Selma's house

Kate's
house

Leah
Sarandon's
house

Elderberry
Road & shops

Alley

Po's
house

Eleanor's
house

Canterbury
College

Friday, April 30

PROLOGUE

The thick tangle of branches made it hard to get down to the path from here, but it was a good choice for the meeting—well hidden from the bridge. Not many joggers picked this part of the path to run on, even though it was officially a part of Riverside Park. They more often chose the east side where manicured parkland offered more space and safety. Here the path was almost hidden in the curve of the land and the slight incline, covered with bushes and low hanging trees. But this was a much better choice for tonight, for meeting and settling life's heartaches once and for all.

It had to be resolved, to stop before it started. Right now. Tonight. Or a whole, careful life would be ruined, snuffed out in a single second. Everything lost. And for what? A whim, a faulty anger. A foolish indiscretion?

A spring moon hung low in the sky, partially hidden by thin gauzy clouds that drifted slowly by. An eerie light fell on the bridge and through the railings down to the water's edge—pale streaks that fell on the moving water. There was a wind tonight, and it whipped across the water, stirring it up into miniature waves that slapped rhythmically against the shore. From here, protected by the brambles and the bridge and on the less-traveled side of the park, the sounds of the city seemed far away and all that was real was the river and the sky, and the two figures about to meet on the path.

The crunch of gravel was startling at first, then a welcome sound. The aloneness had been oddly frightening. Even the presence of the enemy was welcome.

At last, in minutes, perhaps, the awful fear that had bubbled up and grown into an unbearable weight would go away. With one hand pressed against the beating of an anxious, hopeful heart, the lone figure stepped out of the shadows and smiled into a familiar face.

CHAPTER 1

Wednesday, April 28

This Bouillabaisse a noble dish is,
A sort of soup or broth, or brew,
Or hotchpotch of all sorts of fishes,
That Greenwich never could outdo.
—W. M. Thackeray

"Picasso, you've outdone yourself."

Portia "Po" Paltrow dropped her white napkin beside the plate and looked up into the chef's beaming face. His nose, slightly out of proportion to his face, seemed perilously close to her own. Po pushed back slightly in her chair.

"It is my Mama's recipe," the chef said proudly.

"I had fish tacos once, never fish soup. This is very cool. Like who would have thought?" Phoebe Mellon, a diminutive young mother of toddler twins, rose from her chair and planted a quick kiss on Picasso's sweaty cheek.

"Bouillabaisse," Picasso corrected, clearly pleased at the attention. His fingers squeezed together and pulled the words from his lips like a string of molasses. "Bool-eh-baze, mon amie."

"Bouillabaisse," Phoebe repeated. "Cool." She headed off toward the ladies' room and a quick cell phone call to check on husband Jimmy and the twins.

"It's quite a feat to make good bouillabaisse in the heart of Kansas," Eleanor Canterbury said, wiping a trace of soup from the corner of her mouth. "But you've done it, indeed, dear Picasso." In her 82 years of living life to the fullest, Eleanor had traveled the world several times and eaten bouillabaisse in every coastal village in France. She declared Picasso's among the best, the blend of saffron, orange zest, and crushed fennel seeds balanced perfectly. "Even Venus would be proud," she said.

"Venus who? Venus the goddess?" Kate Simpson lifted her head from scooping up the last spoonful of soup from the wide blue bowl.

Eleanor nodded her gray head of hair, swept up today and held in place with a large, sparkly comb. "It's said Venus served bouillabaisse to her husband Vulcan, to lull him to sleep while she consorted with Mars." She smiled up at Picasso. "Your soup has a rich history, Picasso."

For an instant, the proud smile slipped from Picasso's face. His smooth pink brow pulled together in a grimace.

"Picasso, are you all right?" Po asked.

Picasso gripped the back of Phoebe's empty chair and pulled his smile back into place. "I am excellent, mon amie," he said. "And so is my soup—the fish is flown in fresh on Mondays,

Wednesdays, and Fridays. And those are the only days you will see bouillabaisse on my menu. Never," he wagged his index fingers in the air, "never, *ever* a Tuesday or a Thursday. The fish need to jump from the packed ice right into my pot."

Kate took a hunk of French bread from the basket and soaked up the last remnant of rich broth from the bottom of her bowl. A tiny strand of saffron clung to the bread. "How many pounds do you think we've collectively gained since Picasso came into our lives?" She looked around the table, her eyebrows arched high.

"Horrible thought," Maggie Helmers groaned, pushing away her plate. "Picasso, you're killing us with this fancy French food." But the look of delight on Maggie's face indicated she wasn't about to stop any time soon.

Picasso beamed. The French Quarter, his tiny French bistro, had filled the once-empty storefront on Elderberry Road for a scant six months, but it was lively and thriving, a favorite neighborhood spot, and the Queen Bees quilters occupied the round white-clothed table in the back corner far more often than they cared to admit. They loved the small eatery with its tile floor, tightly packed tables, and yellowing framed photographs on the walls—and they were equally fond of the small round Frenchman who had become a part of their lives.

"We're really here on business. Justification for our decadence," Leah Sarandon said. A professor at nearby Canterbury College, Leah was a dedicated member of the Queen Bees and together with Susan Miller, one of the creative forces in the group. "We're here to talk about the quilt we're making for you, sweet man. We picked Wednesday night because we thought the place would be empty, but look at it—" She gestured to a packed room. "Nearly every table filled."

Picasso scanned the bistro. A thick oak bar curved along the east wall, separated from the dining room by a row of low ferns. His bistro had become a gathering place for drinks after work, a cozy alternative to the downtown bars. Small tables for two lined the row of ferns, and on most nights, like tonight, they were filled. The bar bustled with light chatter. He noticed the mayor at one of the small tables. And nearby, Max Elliott, his lawyer and friend, sat with the president of Canterbury College, sharing a plate of escargot. He was glad to see Max back in the restaurant. The last time he had come in for dinner, the young waiter, Andy Haynes, had dumped a plate of creamy wild mushroom fricassee directly onto his lap. Laurel had been standing directly behind Andy, and Picasso suspected her presence had unnerved the young man. But Max had been a good sport about it. "It's good. It's good," Picasso said, mentally assessing the evening's profits.

Po smiled. "It's good for you, good for the Elderberry neighborhood, and certainly good for us."

Phoebe returned to the table and flopped down in her chair. "My Jimmy is beginning to wonder if Picasso has some secret hold on me."

Picasso threw up his chubby hands in mock horror. "Do not let me be the cause of marital discord, sweet Phoebe."

"Marital discord?" Laurel St. Pierre walked over to Picasso's side and rested one elegant hand on her husband's round shoulder. Laurel was a perfect long-stemmed rose to her husband's daisy. Silky red hair swept her slender shoulders, and her graceful body rose several inches above Picasso's portly frame. Extravagantly high, narrow heels, accentuated her height.

"Well, certainly not yours, Laurel," Po said. She smiled at the lovely hostess.

"Certainly not," Laurel echoed. The smile that followed was distracted, Po thought, and she wondered briefly if Laurel was feeling all right. "Laurel," she said aloud, "Would you like to sit with us for a moment?"

Laurel's eyes scanned the small crowded restaurant, taking in the two couples next to the quilters, a family back in the corner, the small bar tables of business people relaxing with a Scotch and soda before heading home. She spotted Max Elliott, and just the sight of him caused her stomach to churn. Causing Andy to spill the food on Max was a terribly childish thing to do, she thought. But she hadn't been able to control the impulse, seeing him there. It had made her furious. Max Elliott was an enemy, whether he knew it or not, and he deserved far worse than shrimp on his lap. Laurel focused back on Po and forced a smile in place.

"Thank you, Mrs. Paltrow. I'd love to sit with you, but as you can see, we're very busy tonight. I wouldn't want Picasso to fire me," she teased.

Picasso shook his head. "I tell her not to work. But sometimes she doesn't listen to me."

Laurel smiled at her husband, every bit twenty years her senior, then turned away and stopped Andy to point out an empty glass. Andy looked at her adoringly, then hurried off to do her bidding, and Laurel walked back toward the hostess station.

"I think Andy Haynes has a crush on your wife," Kate said, nodding toward the blond-headed waiter servicing the next table. "I used to baby sit for him. He's a sweet boy, though very young and naive."

"And he is a good worker. But you are right, Kate. He follows Laurel around like a pup. But then, should he not? She is a beautiful woman. All my helpers here, they think she is wonderful."

Kate suspected it was mostly the male helpers, but she kept her words to herself and glanced over at Laurel. Andy had found his way back to the hostess's side, and she noticed that Laurel touched his white jacket, straightening the lapel, and smiled up into his young face. She's flirting with him, Kate thought. Poor kid—he will have some trouble digging out from under this crush.

"So, my lovelies," Picasso said beside her. "Tell me about my quilt. How is it coming?"

Kate reached into her large purse and pulled out a stack of pictures. She scattered the pictures across an empty space in the middle of the table. "Okay, Picasso—here's my contribution. Plump and perfect fish."

Picasso leaned over and looked at the photos, then clapped his hands excitedly. "Kate, these are most certainly worthy of my bouillabaisse." Kate's studies at Canterbury College included a photography class, which she was enjoying with a relish she usually reserved for food and arguing with P.J., an old high school flame who had recently come back into her life with an unexpected vengeance.

"These are the fish that inspired the design," Susan explained. At 39, Susan had gone back to school herself, and was refining her natural talent in pursuit of a degree in fiber arts. "The quilt will have an enormous pot at the bottom, and we're recreating these lovely fish in beautiful colors. It will be wonderful in this room."

"I still think doing an appliquéd quilt is going to

19

drive me to drink," Maggie Helmers declared. "I hate appliqué, friends. Those little tiny pieces will make me crazy." Maggie found great solace in being a member of the Queen Bee Quilters. It was her therapy, she often said. A time away from her thriving veterinary clinic to refresh her spirit and send her back to caring for Crestwood's pets with renewed love and vigor. But her quilting experience was limited to backing small shapes with freezer paper, then sewing them up on her mother's old machine. But no matter what she did, her quilting friends helped her make it look beautiful. Appliqué, however, was a little too far out of her comfortable box.

"Mags," Leah said, "I understand how you feel. But I promise, the pieced background demands your special touch. You won't touch a piece of appliqué."

Maggie sighed with relief and took a sip of the wine Picasso had graciously sent over to their table earlier.

"So, Picasso, what do you think?" Po asked.

The Queen Bees quilting group had created many quilts in its thirty-year history. Members moved away or died, and daughters or friends were added, but the love and passion for the art was a staple and was passed along seamlessly. When Picasso asked for a quilt to hang in his restaurant—a tribute to his mother—they had agreed instantly.

Picasso beamed in delight as he looked at the pictures. "Les poisson will fly across the fabric beneath the magic of your lovely fingers!"

A short distance away, Laurel St. Pierre surveyed the room, her slate blue eyes glancing back into the kitchen through the round window in the door, then to the front door. She glanced at her watch. It was early. Laurel took a slow, deep breath and rotated her shoulders beneath the green silk jacket. She looked again at the group of women sitting across the room. They were gesturing excitedly, moving the photographs around, chatting.

Her eyes settled on Kate and she frowned. Kate Simpson. Memories crushed down on Laurel painfully, and she pressed her long fingers against her temple. The headaches were beginning again. She squeezed her eyes shut then opened them again, focusing on anything to take away the pain.

Picasso was still at the table, wedged in between Kate and Portia Paltrow, leaning over the pictures with a look of utter delight on his plump face. His hair was thinning, she noticed, small wisps of brown scattered across the top. Foolish old man, she thought. Boring, silly Frenchman. Laurel brushed her hand across her forehead, staring intently at the hunched figure of her husband. She'd actually loved him once. Or had she? He'd certainly been good to her, scooping her up from a dreadful life—a horrible waitressing job in New York and that dreary fourth floor walk-up. He'd given her a home, more money than she had ever dreamed of, everything she needed to turn from a mouse into Laurel St. Pierre, an elegant, beautiful woman. He'd even moved to Crestwood when she wanted to get away from the city. He had been so useful. Necessary even. But that was about over now. The score was even, or almost so. And then she would move on and finally begin her life. Laurel looked again at Picasso and her lips tightened, her head throbbing.

Look at you standing there, your forehead sweaty, your tummy bulging beneath that awful apron. The words floated inside Laurel's pained head, an uninvited, disturbing chant. *Oh, Picasso, I wish you were dead.*

CHAPTER 2

When Kate and Po left Picasso's bistro a short while later, the sky had darkened and a soft breeze stirred the new buds on the trees lining Elderberry Road. Kate looped her arm through Po's and the two walked slowly down the street toward Po's car.

Although Po herself stood five feet seven in her bare feet, Kate was two inches taller. Her auburn hair, streaked with bronze, hung thick and shiny about her shoulders. Tonight she wore shiny champagne-colored slacks that hugged her hips, a simple black t-shirt, and had thrown a sweater carelessly across her shoulders, knotting the arms in front.

Po turned her head to look at Kate, and thought, as she often did, how proud Liz Simpson would be of her only child. She's decent and kind, Po thought—if a bit unpredictable. And she's totally oblivious of the fact that strangers sometimes stop on the street to look at her, wondering if they've seen her in some romantic comedy with Richard Gere or George Clooney.

"Why doesn't everyone live in Kansas in the springtime?" Kate said, interrupting Po's thoughts. She looked up at the clear spring sky. The big dipper hung low, nearly close enough to touch, Kate thought. Or to jump right in and take a ride.

Po laughed. "You escaped doing it for several years, if memory serves me right. And very happily so!"

Kate's journey back to Kansas to care for her mother before she died was intended to be brief, but a year later she was still here, and "still visiting," she insisted to Po whenever the topic of bringing her furniture back from Boston came up.

"I think I always visited in springtime," Kate answered smugly.

At Gus Schuette's bookstore, Kate and Po paused to check out the new books Gus had placed in his window. "Well, will you look at Bill McKay," Kate said, pointing to a poster in the back of the window.

Po peered past a display of Ed Bain mysteries to the picture of Bill McKay, a handsome hometown boy who had gone through school with her daughter, Sophie, before going off to Yale. "My, Billy has certainly made his parents proud, hasn't he?" she said. *Meet the author,* the sign read. And below, Gus had added, *Crestwood's youngest mayoral candidate.*

"Well, he tries." It was a deep voice that answered Po's question, and Kate spun around, nearly landing in the arms of Bill McKay.

"You saying good things about me?" Bill asked, lifting one eyebrow.

Kate laughed. "You're just as conceited as you were in high school, Bill McKay."

"But it looks good on me, right?" Bill shoved his hands in the pockets of his finely tailored pants. "And life itself looks good on you two beautiful ladies. You fine, Po?"

"Doing fine, Billy." As a youngster, Bill McKay was one of those kids parents liked as much as their kids did. Even when he was in trouble, he'd smile in a disarming way that made you forget he'd chased a ball into your garden, crushing all the new daffodils, or thrown your paper into the bird bath three mornings in a row. Po remembered Sophie going to a dance with him and being thrilled that the class president had chosen her. And she also remembered Bill being kind and gentle when the high school crush ended. Somehow they'd even stayed friends, if she remembered right.

"Now, how lucky can a guy be?" Bill McKay said, spreading his arms wide.

"Probably not much more than this, Billy," Kate said. Kate was a lowly freshman at Crestwood High when Bill McKay was the senior boy that every girl in her class fell madly in love with. And getting to know him on equal footing, teasing him now and then, was something Kate found enormously rewarding as an adult. She also thought he was pretty cute.

"So you wrote a book, Billy," she said. "About what?"

"It's nothing. It's kind of an inspirational book for kids," he said. "It's about living in a small town and seeking your dream. Gus is making more of it than it deserves."

"Well, it sounds like you're doing exactly that, Bill—seeking your dreams," Po said. "Your parents must be proud." The McKays had lived for years in Po's comfortable neighborhood, occupying a large and stately brick home that was known by everyone in town as the McKay Mansion. Bill's dad owned several companies in

Crestwood and Kansas City, and commanded great respect from all who knew him, though word had it he wasn't an easy man to work for. Nor, Po suspected, was he an easy man to have as a father. Though Billy had wormed his way into her life, she and Sam were never that fond of the elder McKays.

"They're in Florida most of the time now. Living the good life," Bill said.

"And their businesses?" Po asked.

"I'm handling one—the commercial real estate."

Just then a young woman carrying one of Gus's signature book bags stepped out of the book store and walked over to Bill, sliding into his side. She smiled at Po and Kate.

"Kate and Po," Bill said, "I'd like you to meet Janna Hathaway, my fiancé. Janna, Kate and I went to high school together, and Po is an old friend of my parents and a neighbor. She helped finance my first ten-speed by letting me mow her lawn one summer."

Janna moved closer to Bill, one arm wrapping around his waist. She smiled politely, her eyes lingering for a few seconds on Kate, then focusing back on Bill's face.

Kate observed the young woman with the plain features. Except for her Prada bag and elegant Italian leather jacket, she was the kind of person who could easily get lost in a crowd, her brown hair thin, her nose a little too short, and her eyebrows meeting too close together to emphasize her pretty brown eyes. But mostly she was the opposite of any of the girls Bill McKay had dated, except maybe the underclassmen with whom he flirted, then walked away, unknowingly leaving behind a pile of broken hearts. She was definitely not the beauties who openly sought out Bill McKay with his Kennedyesque aura.

Po was asking about the wedding, and Kate half-listened as Janna explained that the preparations were nearly complete, though the wedding was scheduled for the next spring nearly a year off. She was describing an elaborate wedding that Kate suspected would highlight the social season. Bill seemed slightly embarrassed at the preparations, but listened politely as Janna talked.

"Janna's from St. Louis," Bill said finally, steering the conversation away from the wedding. He wrapped an arm around her shoulders, and Janna seemed to melt into the warmth of his body.

"My father is a banker and investor," she said. "In fact, he'll be doing some business with Bill soon, helping him build his business."

"That's nice," Po said. She watched the three young people: Kate, who wouldn't know a pedigree if it were wrapped around her neck; Bill, whose father had tried to mold his only son in his likeness—disarming good looks and a little too impressed with power and titles and attentiveness to who owned what. But Bill McKay seemed to have avoided some of that, and from all reports, had his head on straight. Janna might be another story, and Po wondered briefly if insecurity caused her to display her family's standing so openly.

"We're building a house out on the east side of town," Bill said to both of them. "Out past Canterbury College. Janna's here for awhile to start the decorating process."

"Kate, you'll have to tell me what Bill was like in high school," Janna said. "Were you friends?" She lifted herself tall on her Manolo Blahnik shoes as she talked.

"Bill knew everyone in school, Janna," Kate said. She looked up at Bill. "You were pretty much everyone's friend, the way I remember it, Billy. I was a lowly freshman, and you even talked to me. Especially around the time of class elections."

Bill laughed. "Well, it worked, didn't it?"

"Every time." And it had, Kate remembered. Bill McKay managed to win every class election, every award, and every girl's heart. She remembered his parents at the honor assemblies, nodding approval in a way that said this was expected of their only son, and nothing less. And when he was accepted at Yale, there was a front-page story in the town newspaper citing his accomplishments. Kate smiled again at Janna, feeling the woman's gaze on her.

"Bill and I were about to get dinner," Janna said, looking up at Bill.

"Oh, you have to go to Picasso's," Kate said, the memory of Picasso's bouillabaisse lifting her voice. She could still taste it on the tip of her tongue. "It's absolutely the best restaurant in Crestwood, bar none."

Janna looked up at Bill. "See? I told you people say it's good." She looked back at Po and Kate. "Bill never eats in a restaurant until it's been operating for one year. A McKay rule, he tells me." Janna laughed lightly.

"Well, then he's foolish and will miss out on something special," Kate said. She grinned at Bill.

Bill looked at Janna and smiled in a way Kate remembered well. "I had my heart set on Mexican tonight," he said.

"That sounds good to me, too," Janna said immediately.

"And I'll take you to France on your honeymoon," Bill added. "Will that make up for it?"

Janna giggled like a schoolgirl, though Kate suspected she was older than Billy. On the one hand she seemed to melt in the presence of her fiancé. On the other, she seemed to have some kind of a hold on the relationship. But then, Kate thought, what relationship didn't reveal some inconsistencies, once you peeled off a layer or two?

"Guess I'd better go feed my bride-to-be," Bill said. "But it sure is good to see you two." He smiled at each of them, then nodded at Gus's poster and shrugged. "And hey, your votes would be welcome, you two."

"And knowing you, Bill, you'll charm me into my vote once again," Kate said.

Bill's face turned serious. "Thanks, Kate. But I've grown up a little bit—or at least I hope I have. I still want your vote, but hope you'll give it to me because I want to do good things for Crestwood." He smiled again, then nodded to each of them, and walked on down the street.

"He's gonna get it, too," Gus Schuette said, coming out and standing on the step outside his door. He watched Bill and Janna disappear around the corner.

"Think so?" Po asked.

"No question in my mind. He's a good man."

"I think you may be right, Gus," Po said. "Billy has turned out well, and maybe in spite of those ambitious parents of his."

"I've volunteered to help him out some. Arrange some gatherings, that sort of thing. And you'd think I'd have lassoed the moon for him, all the thanks he's pouring on me."

"That's sure nice of you, Gus," Kate said. Gus Schuette was a good man to have on your side, she thought. He knew everyone in town, and beneath his sometimes grumpy exterior, he was a fine man and well respected. "I've always liked Billy, but if push comes to shove, I think *you'd* make a mighty fine mayor, Gus Schuette." Kate poked him gently in the ribs.

Po laughed as Kate blew Gus a kiss, and the two women bid him good-night and walked on down the street.

Gus stood on the step in the moonlight, scratching his chin. *Hmmm,* he thought, turning to inspect his reflection in the glass. *Mayor, eh?*

CHAPTER 3

"Po, I'm addicted." Kate dropped her backpack on a chair in Po's kitchen and walked toward the refrigerator. She opened the stainless steel door and peered inside. "All I want to do is take pictures. Heck with grading papers, writing papers, going to school." She pulled out a bottle of water and looked over her shoulder at her godmother.

Po was sitting at the wide wooden table paying bills, comfortable in a pair of jeans and light blue turtleneck sweater. Spring sunlight poured through the back windows and across the spacious kitchen and family room. It had been warm enough today to open the windows a crack, letting crisp breezes clean out the staid winter air. Po looked over the top of her glasses at Kate. "You're very good at it, you know. Your mother would be so proud of you, Kate."

Kate laughed and walked across the kitchen. She pulled out a chair across from Po and sat down, propping her elbows on the thick table. "You say that about everything I do, you sweet thing you."

"Not about your quilting. You're not very good at that." Po patted Kate's arm.

"But—" Kate lifted one brow and waited. Her enormous brown eyes focused intently on Po, tugging out a compliment.

"But you're trying," Po said. "And you're getting a little better."

"Now don't get carried away." Kate's throaty laughter warmed the large comfortable kitchen. It had been a second home to her since she was born. And after her mother died, it became even more of a haven, a place to be with her mother's best friend, a place to be safe, a place to be Kate.

"You know, Po, I think I'll actually be more successful with this new kind of quilt we're doing for Picasso."

"Because it involves food?" Now Po laughed.

"Well, that, too," Kate admitted. At nearly five foot ten, Kate's long slender body handled food nicely, distributing it on her lanky frame without ever turning to fat. "I like the appliqué idea, Po. No matter what Maggie says. I think I'll be better at that than trying to line up points."

"Some quilters like it, some don't. We'll see. It isn't easy, Kate."

Kate took an apple from the large wooden bowl on the table. She rubbed it absentmindedly. "Picasso seems thrilled with the whole idea. But did you notice Laurel last night?"

"I did. She seemed worried."

"Or angry. I caught her looking at all of us once, and there was fire in those gorgeous eyes."

Po nodded. "I saw something there, too. Perhaps she thinks we're bad for business, taking up that big round table so frequently." Po closed her checkbook and set down her pen.

"Po, there's something about Laurel that throws me off kilter. You know that feeling of déjà vu you sometimes get? I swear I've met Laurel St. Pierre before."

"In Boston, maybe? Picasso said they met on the east coast. New York, I think."

"No, I asked her. She's never been to Boston, and she seemed insulted when I said I thought I knew her. She's strange, Po. I think—"

The rattle of the back door stopped Kate's words mid sentence.

"Hi, beautiful ladies." P.J. Flanigan walked through the kitchen door and across the room. He leaned over Po and planted a kiss on her cheek. A hunk of brown hair fell across his forehead. Then he rounded the table and stood behind Kate. Bending at the waist, he whispered into her ear from behind, his nose tickling her cheek. "Where've you been all my life?"

33

"Just here. Waiting. Waiting for Flanigan," Kate answered, twisting her body to look up into his face.

"Hmm, catchy title. Think I'll write a play about that. Waiting for Flanigan." P.J. straightened up and headed for Po's collection of bright thick coffee mugs displayed behind a glass cupboard door. "As lovely as you two are," he said over his shoulder, "I'm really here on business." P.J. filled his mug with coffee. "We had a strange thing happen last night at the department. I thought maybe you could shed some light on it."

"What's that?" Kate took a bite of her apple and watched P.J. as he helped himself to a muffin from Po's bread container. P.J. was as comfortable in Po's kitchen as she was. He had known the Paltrows all his life. And Kate knew that the young lawyer-turned-policeman loved Po—a fact that fueled all sorts of other feelings that were beginning to play around inside her whenever P.J. came into a room.

"A domestic violence call," P.J. said, scattering Kate's thoughts. "And it was from Laurel St. Pierre."

"No!" Kate and Po's voices collided in the kitchen's coffee-scented air.

"Yep. About 1 a.m. I wasn't there, but Frank Stangel—a buddy—said it was very strange. He got the call, and when he and his partner got to the St. Pierres', they found Mrs. St. Pierre sitting

34

on the front step of the house, their big place over on Willow Street. Laurel was crying her eyes out. No bruises, but she was very distraught."

"And Picasso?" Kate asked.

"Nowhere to be found."

"That doesn't make sense, P.J.," Po said. "Picasso is a fine man. And gentle as a lamb. What's more, he adores Laurel." Worry creased her forehead.

"I guess we don't know what goes on behind closed doors, do we?"

"We saw them both last night at the restaurant," Po said.

"Kate mentioned you were going to the French Quarter last night." P.J. took a bite of the blueberry muffin and washed it down with a swig of coffee. He looked from one woman to the other. "Did you notice anything different in the restaurant?"

Kate and Po were silent for a moment, thinking back over their delicious dinner of bouillabaisse and crusty French bread. Both seemed reluctant to repeat their recent conversation about Laurel. It was one thing to gossip among friends, another to lay it all out for a policeman's eyes to dissect. Even if that policeman was P.J.

"Laurel . . ." Kate began cautiously.

"Seemed distracted," Po finished. "But Picasso was his usual happy self, and affectionate toward Laurel the way he always is. No, this doesn't make sense. Did you ever find Picasso?"

35

"Yep. Cruiser spotted him walking along the river path about dawn. Had his apron on and all. Said he'd been at the restaurant—"

"In the middle of the night?"

"He said he sometimes does that. He seemed shocked that Laurel had called the police. They'd had an argument, he said, that's all. And he'd gone back to the restaurant to 'cook it off,' as he put it. Then decided to take the long way home to relax himself."

"And?"

"That's it. But Laurel claimed more than an argument, though no one saw signs to validate it. Said she was afraid of him and couldn't we do something?"

"Afraid of Picasso? That is absolutely ridiculous!" Po shook her head and pushed her glasses up into her gray-streaked hair. At sixty-one, Po knew everyone in town, and her opinions of Crestwood's residents were reliable and thoughtful. "He hasn't lived here that long, true, but I know an honest, kind man when I see one. Picasso is a friend."

"It's odd. For sure," P.J. said. "I always thought he was a nice guy, too. Don't care for that fancy French food much, but he's always happy to make me a steak."

"Such plebian taste," Kate said, resting one hand on P.J.'s muscular arm. "What do Po and I see in you?"

36

P.J. pushed his chair closer. "Boyish charm, I suspect." He grinned over his coffee mug.

Po watched the two and her chest constricted slightly. She couldn't have instigated this evolving relationship better herself, though she surely would have tried if it didn't seem to be happening on its own. Kate was resisting, she knew, not sure she was ready to plant any roots down in Crestwood, Kansas. But Po had known both P.J. and Kate since they were babies, and she thought Crestwood roots were just fine.

Kate stood. "This mess with Picasso upsets me," she said. "There has to be another side to the story." She pushed a handful of hair behind her ear and walked over to the sink.

"There usually is." PJ took a long swallow of coffee. "Great brew, Po."

"So what do you do now?" Po asked.

"Nothing. But there's a record of it now. So if there's a next time, it will make a difference in how we look at it. But for the present, it's 'he said, she said.'"

"And she must be wrong." Kate rinsed out her mug and put it in the dishwasher.

"Spoken with pure objectivity," P.J. said.

"Intuition," Kate snapped back. "And if you think Picasso could ever hurt anyone, P.J. Flanigan, you're dead wrong. He's a prince. And you can tell your buddies at the department that."

"Whoa," P.J. said, getting up from the table.

"Don't get your dander up, Katie. They're just doing their job."

Kate softened. "I suppose." She checked her watch and picked up her backpack, flinging it over one shoulder. "Well, I have a date with a professor to talk about cameras, so I'm out of here. You two have a good day."

Kate blew a kiss across the room, then disappeared out the back door.

"Interesting young woman," P.J. said, watching her leave.

Po laughed. "Yes, P.J. I guess you could say that."

"But she may be wrong about Picasso, Po. The guys at the station found Laurel St. Pierre mighty convincing."

"That's too bad. I think they were fooled, P.J. I don't mean to speak ill of her, but I think Laurel has a bit of the actress in her."

P.J. shook his head and walked over to the sink to rinse out his cup. "You're as stubborn as Kate is, Po. Just be careful, is all I ask."

"Be careful? P.J., now I think it's you who has the dramatic streak. Be careful of a sweet French chef with a heart as big as his amazing mousse au chocolat? Shame on you!"

But after P.J. left, Po sat alone at the kitchen table, her bills in a neat stack next to her pen, and her mind wandering back over conversations she had with Picasso in recent days. A spring wind had picked up and beat the branches of her

38

willow tree against the side of the house. He'd seemed worried about something, but when Po asked if everything was all right, he'd pushed a smile back across his round face and assured her he was fine. Life was fine, he had said. And if not perfect, he confided to Po, he could live with it.

Live with *what,* Po wondered now.

CHAPTER 4

Kate's camera hung loosely from her neck, moving rhythmically as she jogged slowly along the river path in the newly built Riverside Park. The park ran along both sides of the Emerald River, a meandering stretch of water that curved its way through the center of the small hilly town. Wide bridges anchored it at either end, with one in the middle.

The park had been talked about for as long as Kate could remember—her own father, Jim Simpson, had spearheaded a group of town leaders, forging the way for the acres of green that now hugged the sides of the river.

Dad would have loved this, she thought. A wide paved path, dotted with gaslights, and clusters of comfortable benches curved along the entire length of the park. Small walking paths spread out from the main lane on the east side of the river like a spider web, meandering back into clumps of trees and picnic tables and play areas with sandboxes and swings. The bridges provided the perfect place to stand and watch small kayaks and paddle boats go up and down the river. On the west side of the river, the same continuous path, connected by a bridge, ran all the way to the small Crestwood downtown, but the park itself was less developed, more rugged. In a month, the summer concerts would start in the gazebo up near the bridge, and the park would be teeming with people, the bridges crowded, the smell of hotdogs, beer, and lemonade filling the air.

But today the park was quiet, with just a smattering of walkers, a few mothers pushing strollers, and some children just out of school chasing a kite up on the hill. Kate came to a stop beside a wooden bench, cemented into the cobbled path. She bent at the waist and stretched her hands down toward the ground, then sat down and breathed deeply.

"Hey, Miz Simpson, what's up?"

Kate looked up into the grinning face of Amber King, a student in the senior English class in which Kate substituted often. "Hi, Amber. What are you doing here?"

Amber flopped down on the bench beside her and pointed to her backpack. "I hang out here and people watch. Fodder for my writing." She looked at Kate's camera. "Looks like you do the same."

Kate lifted the camera up, focused on Amber, and snapped it a few times. "I guess you could say that," she said. "I like watching people through this lens—you see them in a whole new way. Sometimes I almost feel like a voyeur. Take a look."

Amber took the camera, held it in front of her, and looked through the small square viewer. She focused on the river and a family of goslings slowly heading downstream. Then she shifted on the bench and snapped away at the scene behind her, a young mother and her baby lying on their backs on the side of the hill, and further up, capturing a couple as entwined with one another as the clump of trees behind them

Kate watched Amber as she pivoted on the bench. She was zooming in now on the loving couple up on the hill, snapping a sequence of shots. Kate wondered if she had been that sure of herself at 17. The kids she taught fascinated her, and though substitute teaching had never been on her list of things she wanted to do in life, she was discovering that she liked it. The chance opening when she returned to Crestwood last year had filled a need for both her and the high school. Returning to the same wide halls that housed four years of her life was a nostalgic trip. Some of the teachers who had taught Kate were still there, including Betsy Carroll, a favorite guidance counselor who had spent much of her time

41

keeping Kate on the straight and narrow. She enjoyed the time she now spent with Betsy, speaking adult to adult. And then there were kids like Amber, who made her think she might sign on again next fall if there was a need.

"Very cool camera, Miz Simpson. Digital is the way to go. And the way for me to go is up that yonder hill to ponder the poetry of Yeats." Amber stood and handed the camera back to Kate. "I will leave you alone to your voyeuring."

Kate chuckled and watched Amber saunter up the path, find a grassy spot and settle down. Kate followed her through the camera's eye, then panned across the hilltop to the couple standing close in the shade of the trees. It was a camera-perfect sight—dark green trees, a neatly mulched path, and two entwined figures cloaked in the shadows and lost in a passionate embrace. She lowered her camera to her lap and squinted at the two figures. There was something frighteningly familiar in the stance of the woman, her hands now on her hips. Kate stared hard, and watched as the couple moved another step apart. They seemed to be talking, gesturing. And while Kate continued to stare, the woman lifted her arm and slapped the man forcefully across the face. In the next instant, they moved beyond the trees and out of Kate's view.

Kate stood and lifted her camera from her neck. "Well, I'll be," she muttered. Maybe voyeuring isn't all it's cracked up to be. She slipped the camera into a small leather case, strained unsuccessfully to catch another glimpse of the couple, then turned and headed toward her home.

"I swear it was Laurel St. Pierre," Kate said. "And she was very, very cozy with some tall, dark stranger. Then all of a sudden, the embrace dissolved and she whacked him one."

Kate, Po, and Eleanor Canterbury sat on Po's back deck, sipping martinis in the diminishing daylight. Kate had kept the disturbing scene in the river park to herself for 24 hours, but wrapped in a sweater and ensconced in the comfortable Adirondack chair on Po's wide, comfortable deck, Kate blurted out what she had seen.

The early-evening martini ritual—or sparkling water for those who preferred it—was something Po's friends could count on—a place and time to unwind, to sit quietly in the company of a friend, or sometimes, like today, to sort through disturbing news.

"I believe you, Kate," Po said. "But perhaps it was an innocent, chance meeting. Perhaps she was out for a walk and ran into an acquaintance. An old friend. Or . . ."

"Po, she was kissing him on the lips!" Kate paused and replayed the brief incident in her mind. It had been strange. First the couple was pressed together as if a giant vice had squeezed their bodies tight, and then suddenly arms flailed angrily.

"He was tall," Kate said. "Definitely not Picasso. But it was so hard to see. They were standing in shadows."

"We know so little about Laurel," Eleanor said. She pushed a loose strand of gray hair behind one ear. Eleanor lived a stone's throw from Po, just at the edge of the college named after her deceased husband's family, and she often walked by Po's on nice evenings, her cane tapping out a familiar rhythm in the tree-shaded neighborhood. Sometimes Po worried about her walking alone, but Eleanor insisted the hand-carved cane she'd picked up at a market in Spain was weapon enough should anyone give her trouble. "As if they would," she'd laugh in her gravely way.

"Laurel is a troubled young woman," Eleanor said now. "There's a pain behind those pretty eyes. I see it sometimes when she's working in the restaurant. And I saw her at Wally's drugstore one day when I was picking up my vitamins. She was asking Wally about a stronger medication for pain. When I approached her, she told me she had headaches sometimes, but just between the three of us, I think the pain comes from another place."

"That may be true, Eleanor," Kate said. "And you're a compassionate soul. But it's Picasso I care about."

"We all do, Kate," Po said. "But what goes on between a couple is their business."

"Oh, phooey, Po. You sound just like my mother. I think you two spent far too much time together. If Picasso is having trouble, I don't care who it's with, I want to help him. And I don't trust Laurel St. Pierre for a single second." Kate took a drink of her Pellegrino. The clink of ice cubes was loud in the quiet evening air. "There's something about her, I don't know. Like she's looking at me, waiting for me to say something to her. It's strange. And, frankly, I don't want her messing with Picasso's heart."

Po got up and flipped a switch that lit a low row of gaslights bordering the edge of her deck. They flickered on, bright against the darkening night. She paused behind Kate's chair and rested one hand on her shoulder. "But Kate, dear, what it comes down to is this: there's not a thing you can do about it."

After Kate and Eleanor left, Po went inside, slipped a Nora Jones CD into the player and tried to finish an article she was writing for the Sunday magazine on crazy quilts. But thoughts of Picasso kept drifting in and out of her mind, scattering the descriptions of the quilt form's utilitarian beginnings, and then its evolvement into a hobby for well-to-do women, who spent their days piecing together expensive silk and satin pieces of fabric and embroidering intricate, lovely designs. That was a world away, she thought. Today women rarely had the time or the luxury to devote to such pastimes. They were running children to soccer games or band practice—or helping husbands manage restaurants.

Po had seen a change in Picasso in the past few weeks. His ready smile had a droop to it, his chuckle was a little more forced. And even his interest in the quilt they were fashioning for the back wall of his restaurant seemed a little distant, less exuberant. Did this liaison, or whatever it was that Kate encountered, have something to do with it?

But she needed to take her own advice, she decided. She had too many things on her own plate to get involved, uninvited, into someone's personal problems. Po stared at the screen on her computer. What was her business was finishing this article.

But writing came in fits and starts, and when Po finally decided to go to bed a few hours later, she fixed herself some sleepy time tea first. Somehow she anticipated sleep would be as difficult as the writing had been. She couldn't put her finger on the cause. Concern for Picasso? A writing deadline? Or was it just one of those anxious times in life when things aren't as smooth and tranquil as they sometimes are? Her mother had always told her those were the fruitful, creative times, like a plant beneath the soil's surface, just about to burst forth in brilliant colors. Restlessness could be a *good* thing, her mother had insisted.

But Po's optimistic and wise mother never mentioned the other side of restlessness. The dark side that might be the harbinger of distressing events.

Ella Paltrow would never have imagined—not in a million years—that the nagging unrest that kept her daughter tossing beneath her fine cotton sheets that moonless night might have portended a murder.

CHAPTER 5

The next morning came far too early, but a brisk shower brought life back into Po's body. That and the thought that it was Saturday morning and she'd be spending it, as usual, with the remarkable Queen Bees. She slipped into light slacks and a cotton blouse, brushed her hair and pulled it back into a knot at the base of her neck, then headed downstairs and out the back door.

Po took advantage of the gorgeous spring day and walked the few blocks from her home to the Elderberry shops. She hoped the crisp air would help her shake the uneasiness that interrupted her sleep. She loved her Saturday mornings and was determined not to let unknown anxiety interfere with her day. It had kept her from rising at five for her morning run, and that was the extent that she would allow it to ruin her day. Po moved aside while two college coeds whizzed by. Exams were not far off and tension was tossed to the wind as they ran down the flowering streets of Crestwood.

The Queen Bees met at Selma's Quilt Shop at eight a.m. every Saturday for their weekly quilting gathering. Not everyone made it each Saturday, but they'd decided a long time ago that meeting monthly didn't do the trick—so sometimes there would be three of them on the weekend morning, sometimes six or eight. Po herself sometimes missed if her daughter Sophie was in town with Po's beloved grandchildren, or one of the boys managed a weekend away from their busy lives in California to visit. Or if she had a book deadline or lecture to prepare. But she found the gathering important to her well-being and was always there if her schedule permitted. She'd been a member of the Queen Bees from its beginning thirty years before, when she was a young bride having babies, teaching writing, and helping her husband Sam up the ladder of academia. Eventually, Sam climbed that ladder to the top—the youngest president in the history of Canterbury College. And the whole town had mourned when a sudden heart attack had taken Sam Paltrow from their lives far too early.

"Sam," Po said softly as she circled a child's

scooter left out on the sidewalk, "You'd like this group. Maggie Helmers—she was in school with Sophie, you remember? And she's now Crestwood's busiest veterinarian. There's a young mom—Phoebe—who is married to Jimmy Mellon. His parents were big benefactors at the college. A bit stuffy, though well intentioned, I suppose. And of course, dear Eleanor Canterbury is still there and never misses a session—unless she's off on an African safari or visiting Egyptian pyramids. I swear, Sam, at 82 she has more wind in her sails than that boat you used to race on Lake Quivira." Po stopped and leaned over a bed of daffodils bordering a thick green lawn. *Lovely,* she thought, then continued on her way. "And Leah Sarandon, of course. She still teaches at Canterbury, still giving the male faculty a hard time, and still remembers the day you promoted her to department head against the wishes of that stodgy board you had to deal with. Susan Miller is another Bee—you didn't know Susan—she was involved in all that mess last year when Owen Hill was murdered, the poor girl. But she has bounced back beautifully and still helps Selma in the shop, even though she inherited a hunk of money from Owen. She's an amazing, talented quilter."

"Hey, Po, who you talking to?" Kate rode up behind Po, braking her bike to a stop. "I called to you but you didn't seem to hear—you were deep in conversation."

Po laughed and brushed a loose strand of hair behind her ear. She pushed her sunglasses to the top of her head and looked at Kate. "Just talking with an old friend, that's all."

Kate got off her bike and began walking next to Po. She looped one arm loosely around her shoulders. "I talk to mom, too. They're still with us, for sure."

Po smiled, waved at a woman across the street, and changed the subject. "You're early for quilting, honey. That's not like you at all."

Kate's throaty laugh, a bit too loud, filled the space between them. "Miracles happen. You're a bit early yourself. Are you hoping Marla has the cinnamon rolls finished?"

"Maybe a cup of coffee. I didn't sleep well." She rotated her shoulders as if to shrug off the last remnants of discomfort that still lay just beyond conscious thought. "I thought maybe Selma might need some help readying the store. Since she started displaying quilts on Friday nights, she's had a mess of people going through the store. Great for business but lots of work."

"That's a good idea to use that west wall of her store for displays. But what we really need is a quilting museum. When I lived on the east coast, we used to visit one in Lowell, a great little town not too far north of Boston. It's an amazing museum, with terrific, passionate quilters, just like us. We could do that here."

"Selma and Susan have similar ideas, I think. They have their eyes on that old brick building across the street." Po and Kate rounded the corner onto Elderberry Road, and Po pointed to a large, three-story building that used to house a hardware store before Home Depot moved into the mall on the edge of town. Today a *For Sale* sign was posted in one of the windows.

Kate squinted to read the sign. "McKay Commercial Real Estate," she read. "Billy's everywhere."

"He's a go-getter, just like his father."

"Well, he charmed the socks off every teacher in Crestwood High," Kate said. "If he's half as good with his clients, he'll be very successful."

"Eleanor told me yesterday that he may give the city a good deal on an old warehouse down near the river. They want to turn it into a half-way house."

"That doesn't surprise me. He was always the one to lead the food drives in high school. And though I don't mean to take away from his generosity, Po, none of that will hurt his political career."

"No, you're right about that." Po nodded to a neighbor walking by. "But if it helps the city in the process, more power to him."

Kate nodded. She was actually proud of Billy, and had to admit she enjoyed the frequent encounters they'd had recently. Janna Hathaway was a very lucky woman, and Kate suspected from the tight grip she kept on Bill, that she was well aware of that fact.

Kate and Po glanced into the window of the antiques store on the corner. A young couple from Kansas City had recently bought the old Windsor House Antiques after a scandal had sent the owner to jail. The formerly dark and elegant store had taken on a bright new look, with skylights and bright urns overflowing with flowers in every window. While it still held some priceless antiques, the store was more affordable now, and Po thought the change was a good one.

Next door, Marla already had customers filling the front bay window of her bakery and café, and the smell of cinnamon drifted out the open door. Daisy Sample, owner of the Elderberry Road florist, Flowers by Daisy, was walking out of Marla's with a huge muffin in her hand as she headed next door to open her own shop. "Morning ladies," she called out and continued on her way.

Brew and Brie, Po's favorite shop for picking up Vermont white cheddar and a good Merlot, was closed up tighter than a drum. "Ambrose and Jesse are getting a late start, as usual," Po said.

They passed by Gus's place and waved as he pulled up the blinds on the front window, readying himself for the Saturday crowd. Next to Gus's, a small open space had been turned into a patio, separating the bookstore from the French restaurant. Gus and Picasso collaborated to add some benches and flower pots, and it became a perfect place to read books from the book store while waiting for a table at the French Quarter—a plus for both owners. At this hour on a Saturday morning, it was deserted, save for a collection of blue jays eating up last night's crumbs.

Po frowned as she looked through the slats of the blinds on Picasso's windows and into the darkness beyond. "It's one thing for Ambrose and Jesse to sleep in, but Picasso is always here at this hour."

"He probably had a late night last night."

"That doesn't matter. He's here every Saturday morning when I jog by. Always." She frowned. "Kate, something's wrong." Po stood still, staring at the front door to the restaurant.

Kate touched her arm. "Po, come on. Everyone deserves to sleep in now and then—even Picasso. I'm late all the time and you never worry. Let's go." She tugged playfully on the sleeve of Po's jeans jacket.

Reluctantly Po began to walk toward Selma's. But she couldn't shake the feeling that she was needed somewhere, and it wasn't at the big oak table in the back of Selma's quilt store.

But before they could walk through the door to Selma's shop, it swung open from the inside. Selma stood alone in the entry, her face as chalky white as the sidewalk, and Po knew without a smidgen of a doubt that she was right.

"Picasso?" Po asked. Her heart was squeezed tightly against the wall of her chest.

Selma shook her head no, then yes. And then she grabbed them each by the arm and drew a confused Po and Kate into the shop.

"Laurel," she said in the softest voice Po had ever heard Selma use. "Laurel St. Pierre is dead."

CHAPTER 6

By the time the remaining Bees arrived at Selma's, Kate had talked to P.J. He quickly confirmed the story already spreading across the small town as people turned on their radios and televisions for the early morning news.

"Laurel St. Pierre," Kate said, returning to the table with her cell phone in her hand. Her tone was hushed and disbelieving. "We were just talking about her yesterday, maybe at the very moment she was being hurled into that river." Kate had told P.J. on the phone about seeing Laurel in the park with a stranger. Similar stories were coming in to the station, he told her. And they'd be checking them all out.

"Like who would do such a thing?" Phoebe's eyes filled her face. "And I'm bringing my babies up in this world? This is total craziness." She fingered one of several earrings curling up the edge of her ear.

"Poor Picasso," Po said. "He adored Laurel. How difficult this must be for him."

"We saw him last night at the restaurant," Selma said. "Susan and I stopped by after closing up the shop. We had had a busy night and thought a slight nip would help us sleep."

"Was Laurel there?" Kate asked.

"No," Susan said. "And it was crowded, being Friday night, so we were a little surprised. But Picasso said he had insisted she take the night off because she'd been working too hard."

"Does anyone know how they found her?" Maggie asked. "The news report I heard on the way over was a little sketchy."

Kate put her mug down. P.J.'s account was more complete than the news, although she knew that he only told her what would eventually be common knowledge, not the whole story. "P.J. said a couple of college kids found her. They were camping near that old quarry where the river starts to bend. P.J. said a large mound of boulders in the river's bend stopped her body from heading toward the Gulf of Mexico. At first they thought she drowned—but there was evidence of a blow to her head, and now they think that was what killed her. They don't know where she entered the river, but they know where she ended up."

"Oh, gross. I need coffee." Phoebe walked over

to the sideboard and brought the glass pot back to fill everyone's mugs. Her size-two jeans hugged her body and a bright green t-shirt, stretched across her chest, proclaimed "I love my twins." A platinum mop of hair, no longer than a finger, framed her pixie face, which today lacked its usual wide grin.

At this time on a normal Saturday morning, the table was filled with a dozen pieces of fabric, the sewing machine was whirring at the side, and laughter and talk filled the sky-lit room. Today the mood was somber and disbelieving.

"I liked Laurel," Leah said. She pulled a tissue from the pocket of her long jeans skirt and absently cleaned her round rimless glasses. Shoulder-length brown hair framed Leah's high cheekbones and, without her glasses, her brown eyes were even larger than usual. Today they were filled with sadness. "She took a women's history class from me last semester. There was something mysterious about her, and I guess because we both came here from the east coast, we had an odd bond, and she would sometimes talk to me after class. Asked me what I knew about Crestwood. What it was like to live here."

"She didn't really talk much to me," Kate said.

"But she watched you," Maggie said. "I'd catch her staring at you in the French Quarter some- times."

Kate looked over at Maggie. "That's strange,

Mags. I felt that sometimes, too—I was just telling Po about it yesterday."

"Oh, pooh, Kate," Selma said. "You're a good-looking gal. Everybody looks at you." She took a sip of her coffee, then set the mug down and continued, "But, now that you mention it, Laurel did seem to people watch more than usual, I'll grant you that. She kept a keen eye on everyone coming in and out of the French Quarter."

"She was a help to Picasso in the restaurant, that's for sure," Po said. "I wonder how he's coping? We need to do something. I think his only family is in France."

"What about Laurel's family?" Kate asked. "I wonder if they've been told."

"Laurel never mentioned family," Susan said. "But I think she grew up near New York."

"I drove by Picasso's house on the way over here," Phoebe said. She settled down next to Kate. "There were police cars in the driveway."

"Maybe in the next couple days we could each take some food by to help with visitors," Po said.

"Cooking for Picasso is a little like singing for Pavarotti," Eleanor said. "But I shall certainly take over a fine bottle of French wine. He'll like that."

"And for today, maybe good therapy for all of us would be to work on Picasso's quilt," Selma said. "There's not much else we can do right now."

The group nodded, and as if some unseen stage director had given a cue, soft cloth bags appeared from beneath the table, the sewing machine was brought to life, and Leah filled the table with brightly colored swatches of fabric.

"Here's what we're doing," she said. "Susan and I have worked it all out. This is not going to be one of our democratic, do-whatever-moves-your-spirit kind of projects." As the most gifted and artistic members of the group, Susan and Leah often led the way, and the rest of the group usually responded well, with only an occasional complaint.

"I've expressed my views on this," Maggie started in.

"Yes, you have. And we don't need to hear them again," Leah said.

"You'll be doing sashes and borders, Maggie, or one of the blocks. Not a bit of appliqué," Susan assured her.

"Ah, there is a God," Maggie said.

"Just when I finally get my lines straight, you do this to us," Eleanor said, looking down at the intricate pattern. "I don't think there's a straight line in the whole quilt."

Susan had used graph paper and colored pencils to sketch the drawing for the quilt. In the center, on the bottom half of the quilt, was a large pot, composed of different shapes of black and gray and silver patterns, pieced together in six small blocks. Above the pot were two large appliquéd fish, their bodies an intricate blend of wavy lines, with small yellow and black circles for eyes. Striped fins were flattened against the scaled bodies, and even the simple sketch was beautiful and intricate enough to draw "ahs" and "oohs" from the quilters. Susan and Leah would each create a fish, and these would be appliquéd on the pieced background.

"This is amazing," Po said. "Picasso will be so pleased."

"It's beautiful," Kate said. "I don't know if I can do this justice."

"You're getting better, Kate," Susan said. "Don't underrate yourself. Your photos inspired those fish."

The mood lightened slightly as the group leaned over the table, studying Susan and Leah's design. Graceful lines of steam curled up from the pot, and the pieced background, composed of subdued blocks of deep greens and purples and blues, held the design in place. Tiny flecks of green and gold, which would be appliquéd on in the final stages, represented the bits of herbs and spices that made Picasso's bouillabaisse unique.

"I can almost smell that amazing soup," Phoebe said.

"Bouillabaisse, Phoebe," Kate said, "bool-a-baise." Her feigned French accent, imitating Picasso, made them all smile.

"Picasso will be so pleased," Po said softly.

"But only if it becomes a reality," Leah said, determined not to let the sadness of the day overwhelm them. "So to work ladies. We've already cut up the pieces and made you each your own block patterns. I know Eleanor will only do her piecing by hand but you can decide for yourself. To work!"

CHAPTER 7

For more years than they cared to remember, Po and Leah Sarandon had met for breakfast at Marla's bakery on Sunday mornings, a habit born of their husbands' love for early-morning golf. While the two men enjoyed fresh breezes walking the greens just east of town, their wives, the twelve years' difference in their ages dissolving instantly in the heat of their shared passion for quilting and books and women's history, shared food. As they savored moist, cheesy eggs with wild mushrooms, or whatever other marvelous concoction Marla had put together for that day, their friendship grew. When Sam Paltrow died, the routine went unbroken, filling an even greater need in Po's life as the power of friendship helped her heal.

And in addition to Marla's culinary talents, she never failed to season Po and Leah's breakfast with a generous dose of gossip. Today the large bakery proprietor was like a cat with a whole nest of mice at the ready.

"Ladies," she gushed in an excited stage whisper, "have I got news for you."

Leah smiled at the familiar greeting, and Po suggested that a cup of coffee would better prepare them for the words fighting to get out of Marla's mouth.

Marla filled their mugs, her black eyes darting around the small bakery café, taking stock of empty plates, filled tables, and her young waitresses, making sure no diner went wanting for service. The room was nearly filled, and soon there would be a line out the door, with waiting customers sitting on outdoor benches reading the Sunday paper or chatting with friends. "Awful news about Picasso's wife," she began. "Just awful." Marla set the coffee pot down on the table and wiped her plump hands on her apron. "I know a young girl like that dying is horrible and all, but you know, he may be better off without her."

"Marla! What an awful thing to say," Po said. "Picasso was crazy about Laurel."

"Doesn't mean she was good for him, Po. She could be nasty as all get out if she didn't like you. Ask Max Elliott—she couldn't stand that sweet man—I saw with my own eyes how she'd be rude to him. But that's not the worst of it. Rumor has it that Mrs. St. Pierre had gentlemen friends who were most definitely not of the

French persuasion." Marla leaned over the table and looked back and forth between the two women. "Daisy Sample saw that woman talking to a man in the alley, very cozy like, not two weeks ago. It wasn't Picasso or Jesse or anyone we know. And believe you me, they weren't talking about the weather."

"Daisy should keep her gossip to herself," Po said. "What in heaven's name does talking to a man in an alley mean anyway? I wouldn't call that incriminating. I've talked to men in that alley myself, Marla, and you never had me romantically linked." Po's words were far more forceful than she felt. Kate's recent encounter over at the River Park had run through her dreams all night long. "We need to support Picasso," she said aloud, "and we need to help him through the funeral, not make burying his wife more difficult for him than it already is."

"Won't be a funeral," Marla said smugly.

Po and Leah looked up at her. Po's brows lifted. "You know that?"

"Heard it from Shelby Harrison. He comes in for a sack of cinnamon rolls every single Sunday morning before going over to his funeral home. Bill McKay and Max Elliott were in here talking business things. They do a lot of that lately. Anyhow, it seems Max handles Picasso's legal things just like he does everyone else's, and he was making sure Picasso's wishes were followed.

So Shelby told him that when the police released the body, he was going to quietly take care of things for Picasso at his funeral home. Quick cremation. No funeral. Exactly like Picasso wanted."

"Well, that's how it will be then. Whatever is best for Picasso," Po said. But the news didn't settle easily in her mind, and she didn't know why. Cremation wasn't an uncomfortable thought to her, but eliminating any kind of funeral was a surprise. What about their family and friends? How would he find closure that way? She hoped for Picasso's sake it was the right decision.

"Well, ladies," Marla said, straightening up and scanning the small room for customers needing coffee or checks, "I say stay tuned. There's more to this story than meets the eye. Trust my words." She spotted the Reverend Gottrey on the other side of the restaurant with his finger in the air, wanting attention, and scurried off, her wide backside miraculously weaving in and out among the tables without incident.

A young waitress appeared almost instantly. "Marla says you need comfort food," she said, and set down two plates heaped with blueberry pancakes and small jugs of Vermont maple syrup off to the side.

Leah smiled. "Marla is absolutely right." She stuck her napkin into the top of her blouse and slathered the top pancake with butter, then poured a thick stream of maple syrup across the top.

"It's far too early for Michigan blueberries," Po observed, reaching for the butter.

"She goes up every July, picks 'em fresh, then freezes 'em," the waitress explained, then disappeared.

Delighted, Kate and Po dug in, concentrating on the plump juicy blueberries that filled the pancakes. But the thoughts connecting the two friends across the blue-checkered tablecloth were not entirely of food or Michigan blueberries, but of a friend alone with his grief. And a beautiful young woman robbed of life far too early.

Later that day, after Leah and Po had parted to go about their Sunday routines, Po sat at her kitchen table, staring at the scraps of material that would magically come together to resemble a cooking pot.

The kitchen and family room in Po's large, airy house was the hub of her life—and most of her friends' lives as well—and though she had a sewing machine in her den, this was the area in which most things got worked out, whether it be problems, bills, or quilts. A large stone fireplace anchored one end of the room and was softened with overstuffed chairs and couches, begging for bodies to curl up and stay awhile. Hoover, Po's ten-year-old Golden retriever, was doing exactly that, looking up now and then to let Po know that he was there if she needed him.

But this afternoon what she needed was to get some things done. The Queen Bees had all taken pieces of Picasso's quilt home to work on. And among the twenty things on her to-do list, that seemed to be the most appropriate task for the day, since thoughts of Picasso were not far beneath the surface anyway.

Leah and Susan had outdone themselves on selecting the fabric, Po thought as she fingered the pieces of cotton. Susan had explained that they wanted the quilt to fit into the casual bistro look of Picasso's restaurant, but they also wanted it to add color to the rough pale wall on which it would hang. They knew from the start that a quilt in a restaurant would get abuse from odors and light and the air, but Picasso wanted it there nevertheless, and said he was going to have an acrylic frame built to protect it.

Po looked at the slender piece of cotton in her hand. The pattern was slight, a wavy line that added more texture than pattern to the piece. She was working on the pot at the bottom. Six pieced blocks would form the round image, its sides glistening with sweat from the broth inside. Leah and Susan were geniuses in picking fabrics that created texture and feeling—even emotion—and the nubby blacks and grays and shiny silver patterns added interest, depth, and dimension to her pot. Amazing, she thought. Amazing women.

But the usual joy she felt in creating art out of small pieces of fabric was missing today. And within an hour, Po had put all her supplies back into the closet and had pulled a frozen blackberry tart out of her freezer. Though she had told herself she would give Picasso a few days with family before stopping by to pay her respects, her resolve was lost in the need to give the small round man a hug and a homemade pastry. She ran a brush through her hair and in minutes was driving the short distance to his house.

As she rounded the corner two blocks from Picasso's house, a tall, familiar figure, burnished auburn hair tossed to the wind, caught Po's eye. She pulled over to the curb and rolled down the car window. "So, Kate, you couldn't wait either?"

Kate stopped in her tracks and walked over to the car. She leaned into the open passenger window. "If you don't mind my slightly sweaty body, I'll ride the rest of the way. Couldn't sleep much last night." She opened the door without waiting for a response and slid onto the front seat. "Can't get that little Frenchman off my mind. And nor can you, it looks like."

Po nodded as she accelerated the car. "I wanted to wait until relatives or whomever Picasso would surround himself with at a time like this were gone. But I couldn't wait." She pulled onto Picasso's street, drove halfway down the block and pulled into a wide brick driveway that curved in a half-circle in front of the stately Tudor home. The only other car in the drive was Picasso's small BMW.

Kate eyed the manicured front lawn, then the tall leaded windows defining the front of the house. "It looks deserted," she said.

"Well, we can always leave the basket on the front step if he's resting. He'll appreciate the thought, I'm sure. And if Laurel's family is here, they can have it for breakfast." Po and Kate got out of the car, and Po lifted the basket holding her blackberry tart out of the back seat.

But before they reached the front door, it was pulled open from the inside and a bedraggled, unshaven Picasso stood in the doorframe, beckoning them in.

"Mes amies," Picasso cried, pulling both women together into a tight hug. He stood slightly apart then, kissing them on each cheek. Finally, without a word, he drew them through the open door, through an elaborate foyer, and into a dark living room.

"How are you, dear," Po asked. "We've all been concerned, but we didn't want to intrude."

Picasso shook his head and gestured for them to sit on one of the brocade loveseats framing the hand-carved walnut fireplace.

"First we need some light." Po walked over to a wall of windows covered with heavy shades and pulled them apart. "There. Sunshine can help the soul heal, Picasso." She sat down beside Kate on one of the loveseats.

Picasso sat opposite them, leaning forward with his forearms resting on his knees. He wore an old pair of sweat pants that Po suspected hadn't been taken off for a day or two. The rumpled figure seemed out of place in the expensively decorated room, a forlorn and lonely man, far older than his forty-nine years.

"What has happened to my life?" he asked them simply. His large brown eyes were wet with sadness.

"This is as bad as it can be, Picasso," Po said. "But we are here, and we will help you through this."

"Have Laurel's relatives left?" Kate asked. "Can we do anything for them?"

Picasso shook his head. "There's no one. No family."

"Laurel had no family?"

"Oui," Picasso said as he rose from the couch. "She was a lonely, lost soul when I met her."

"Well, she certainly blossomed under your love," Po said. "Laurel was a beautiful woman."

"That was so important to her. To be beautiful. She had no money when we met. She was a frail, drab waitress working two shifts, but I made sure she had whatever she wanted to let that beautiful soul flourish—spas and hair treatments and a life that allowed her to shine. I didn't even want her to work in the restaurant—but she wanted to come in once we moved here, just to get used to the town and meet the people, she said."

Kate listened carefully, looking now and then at the enormous painting of Laurel above the fireplace. Drab was a word that could never, even in her imagination, be applied to Laurel St. Pierre. "Was it hard for Laurel to move to Kansas from New York?"

Picasso shook his head vehemently. "No, no. It was hard for me!" He punched his hand into his chest and forced out a small laugh. "I loved New York, I loved my restaurant. I made fistfuls of money, more than in my dreams. But when Laurel came into my life, she wanted a quiet life—she was brought up in a small town, like me. So we found this little place, this empty storefront in this sweet little town. And we've been happy here, mostly—" His voice dropped off and he closed his eyes, shaking his round head slowly.

Po rose from the couch and walked over to where Picasso stood beside the fireplace. She hugged him briefly. "Do not pull away from those who care about you, Picasso."

"That is music to my ears, Po. The police, they ask so many questions. They wonder if Laurel had enemies. Laurel, with enemies? How foolish and silly. There was no one who would hurt her. No one. She was a beautiful flower."

"Do you have any idea what happened, Picasso?"

"Certainment," he said. The French word shot through the air like a bullet, and for the first time that day the spirit of the robust little Frenchman filled the room.

"Yes?" Po prompted.

"I know exactly what happened. It was a vicious robbery. Laurel always wanted much dollar bills in her purse. She then felt secure. So someone robbed her of her money and then the monster killed her."

The words were said with the unflagging assurance that this was, indeed, the only possible scenario. The irrefutable truth.

"And the police, this is what they say?"

"They look for problems, they ask about boyfriends—what an awful thing to ask. They ask about trouble in our marriage. Trouble? I would have died for Laurel. I would have given my life for her."

The quick look that passed between Po and Kate carried a single memory—that of P.J.'s recent news that Laurel St. Pierre had filed a complaint against her husband. And looking back into Picasso's sorrowful eyes, Po heard a conviction as sure as anything she had ever heard that Picasso loved his wife without question.

"I know you loved her, Picasso," Po said softly. "I can't imagine what this must be like for you. But please know you have friends a minute away." Po touched his arm, then joined Kate as they walked toward the door, not wanting to extend their uninvited visit too long.

Picasso switched on the light as they entered the darkened foyer and Kate and Po stopped in their tracks.

There on the wall, directly in front of them, hung a magnificent quilt. "Oh, Picasso—how absolutely gorgeous," Kate said. She took a step closer. The quilt was a collection of brilliant blues and greens and yellows, swirling against a deep purple background, and in the center of the swirls, emerging from the folds of the cloth, was a beautiful bird.

Picasso stood beside the two women, looking up at the quilt.

"Where did you get this, Picasso?" Po asked. "It's amazing."

"It was Laurel's," he said quietly.

"Laurel made this?" Kate asked.

He shook his head no. "It was a gift, she told me," Picasso said. "Laurel cherished it. Often she'd take it down and lay it across the bed, fingering it. I'd often find her there, the quilt across her knees. She fingered it as if it were the most valuable thing in her life. I'd find her fixing small threads that came loose, sewing the edges. She cared for it as gently as the child we could never have.

"I suggested to her once that we put it in the restaurant, but she was very distressed at the thought. She would not consider it. It could be only here, in our home, in this place of honor. And she was the only person who could touch it, she told me."

Po looked at the quilt again, her eyes soaking in the fine detail, the lovely, perfect curves of the wings, the blend of appliqué and piecing, just like they were doing on the quilt for Picasso's restaurant. She stared at the vines that wrapped around all sides of the quilt, twirling and curling like dancing nymphs.

"I am so pleased you like it," Picasso said, watching Po's eyes devour the quilt. "You ladies know so much about quilts. I said once we should invite you all over to see it, but—" Picasso's sentence dropped off, and then he looked up and said, almost apologetically, "—but she said this was private. Not for other eyes."

Po watched him look up again at the quilt. It was almost as if he were seeing images of Laurel in this piece of art that she had loved.

Picasso shook his head sadly from side to side, then walked to the door, holding it open for his guests. He forced a smile to his lips. "Thank you, Kate and Po. Your visit to me today means very much."

Po looked back at the quilt, committing it to memory. Then she accepted Picasso's kiss to each cheek and followed Kate through the front door and down the steps to the car.

"Po, what's wrong?" Kate buckled her seatbelt, her eyes on Po as she sat unmoving behind the steering wheel of the car. Her eyes looked straight ahead, through the windshield, but what she saw seemed to Kate to be very far away. "You look like you've seen a ghost."

Po glanced back at Picasso's house, then strapped her own seatbelt in place and looked at Kate. "Maybe I have, Kate. It's that quilt. I would swear on a stack of Bibles that I've seen it before, and it wasn't hanging on Picasso's wall."

CHAPTER 8

The need to buy groceries and clean her family room before friends arrived for supper kept Po from dwelling on the familiar quilt, though images of the bird were in her mind's eye as she prepared the béarnaise sauce for tonight's fillets and piled buffet dishes on the end of the table for dinner. When P.J. and Kate arrived a short while later, Po sent them out back to manage the grill while she went upstairs to take a quick shower and try to wash away the disturbing thoughts.

"Kate and P.J., you're in charge," she had said to them. "Make sure it's wonderful."

P.J. feigned a bow. "You've any doubts, madame?" He grinned at Po to pull her out of her thoughts, then held the porch door open for Kate and followed her outside while Po retreated upstairs.

"She's just worried about Picasso, P.J.," Kate said, placing the platter of steaks beside the grill.

"Well, she may have something to worry about." He opened the heavy cast iron lid and poked the coals to life that Po had lit earlier. Crimson embers lit up the night.

Kate handed P.J. a long fork and he speared each thick steak and placed it on the grill. "What do you mean, P.J.?"

"I think this doesn't look good for Picasso right now, is all I mean."

"P.J., you're crazy," Kate said. Her fists dug into the sides of her waist to keep her from shoving P.J. right off the edge of Po's porch. The evening air was brisk, and small gaslights dotted the wooded area beyond the deck, casting shadows across the spring lawn.

"Calm, down Kate," P.J. said. His brow was furrowed, and the look of levity that usually lit his face had disappeared. He brushed the top of each steak with a thin layer of butter and olive oil. For a moment the sizzle of fat dripping on the coals was the only noise in Po's backyard. P.J. concentrated on the grill, his eyes not meeting Kate's.

When Kate spoke again, her voice was softer, but still edged with anger. "It's just that Picasso is such a kind, good man," she said. "And if you could have heard him earlier today, you'd never in a million years doubt his love for his wife. And what about the guy I saw in the park with Laurel, P.J.? Why isn't he on the top of your list?"

"We're looking into that, Kate. But we've nothing more than what you've told us. And that's not much. Your description includes half of the county. And others have come forward telling of seeing Laurel with different men—even that little waiter at the restaurant spent time with her. But Picasso is the one she was calling abusive."

"But he loved her more than you can imagine, P.J. I am sure of that."

"I'm not doubting the man's love, Kate. But people sometimes do bad things to people they love. Take you—" He tried to joke her out of the moment. "Look how nasty you're being to me—and God knows you're crazy about me."

But Kate would have none of it. "I think that's one of the things that's desperately wrong with our legal system, P.J. We say people are innocent until proven guilty, but then the news gets out there—and the whole world treats you like you're guilty without any proof whatsoever."

The late afternoon news had startled not only Kate, but anyone who knew Picasso and had ever felt his gracious hospitality in the French Quarter bistro. "A small town restaurateur may have some connection to his wife's murder," the reporter on the Kansas City, Missouri, news channel had announced, and then went on to talk of possible marital discord that an unidentified source had passed the reporter's way.

"I don't know how that story ever got on the news tonight. I guess it's the weekend doldrums—there's nothing else to talk about. But it was all some reporter's conjectures, Kate. The police wouldn't say anything like that at this point."

Kate handed P.J. a cup of wine sauce for the meat. "So the police are convinced Picasso is innocent?" Her unrestrained fists returned to her hips.

"The police aren't convinced *you're* innocent, Kate. The guys assigned to the case are just beginning to look into it. Everyone has to be looked at. The guy in the park—whoever he is— the people in the restaurant. Friends of Laurel's. It was a *murder,* Kate."

"Are you two almost ready with the steaks?" Po called through the screen door. She stepped into the doorway, looking refreshed in pale tan slacks and a black sweater.

"Five minutes max, boss lady," P.J. called back, then turned a row of large white mushrooms on the top burner and brushed them generously with garlic butter. He had become Po's Sunday night barbecue doyen in recent months, a role that originated with Sam Paltrow. For years Sam had welcomed friends and neighbors to his Sunday night suppers, and the tradition continued after his death when force of habit and a yearning for Sam and Po's hospitality brought people to Po's doorstep with a bottle of wine in hand or a freshly baked pie nestled in a wicker basket. Sometimes there was a crowd, sometimes a small intimate group, and sometimes Po herself cancelled it because she had a book deadline or another engagement. But in recent months P.J. had been a regular, a fact Po attributed to Kate's weekly presence. But whatever the reason he came, his barbecue skills were nearly as fine as her husband's had been, and Po took full advantage of it.

"Well, just for the record, P.J.," Kate said, "Picasso is a good man. And I'm not so sure his wife was a perfect person. In fact, I suspect there were plenty of people who wouldn't be terribly sad to have Laurel St. Pierre off their radar screen."

"That's a little harsh, Kate."

Kate was silent. She had no basis for her strong words, but she felt them deep inside of her. Laurel had always made her uncomfortable, and instinct told her there were things about the woman that would surprise all of them, including Picasso.

P.J. looked up from the grill and saw the mix of emotion cloud Kate's face. "It'll be okay, Katie," he said. His voice was gentle now. "If there's something we need to know about Laurel, we'll find it out. Now help me with these steaks so we can fatten you up a bit." He pierced the plump fillets with the fork and piled the meat on a platter, then handed it to Kate. As he piled the mushrooms into a bright blue ceramic bowl, he grinned and winked at Kate, trying hard to force a smile to her lips. "Ah, we make a grand culinary team, Kathleen Anne Mary Simpson. Let's now go inside and accept the well-deserved praises of our hungry guests."

Kate looked at him hard and long, then shook her head and allowed the small smile he was waiting for. "You can be so absolutely irritating, P.J. Flanigan—always seeing all sides of everything. But you make it impossible for me to stay mad at you. And I hate that." She turned and headed for the porch door with the bowl of mushrooms held between her hands. "Fatten me up, my foot," she muttered, and walked into the kitchen.

"Ah, perfectly done, P.J.," Po greeted them, and relieved Kate of her bowl. "I think we'll be a small group tonight." She gestured to the family room where Phoebe sat curled up on the couch with Jimmy and the twins, reading to them about a little boy who gave a moose a muffin. Gus Schuette and his wife Rita sat with Eleanor, debating the merits of martinis. Rita was a definite asset to any gathering, her keen wit and outspoken opinions fodder for lively conversation.

"Max Elliott said he'd be by, too, so let's wait a couple more minutes," Po said. She'd been happy when Max called, and hoped there'd be a moment or two to ask him subtly about Laurel St. Pierre. She was surprised at Marla's gossip—she hadn't known Max even knew Laurel. Besides, the thought of anyone not liking Max Elliott was difficult to imagine.

As if on cue, a knock at the front door announced Max's presence. "I've brought a couple more friends," he called from the door, then walked on in. "Knew you wouldn't mind."

"Of course not, Max, now get on in here where I can see that handsome face of yours," called Po.

Max entered the family room, assisted by a short cane that was the only sign of a serious car injury the year before. "Folks, you all know Bill McKay—and his lovely fiancé, Janna." Max bowed toward the woman standing beside the imposing Bill McKay.

"Of course we do. Welcome," Po said warmly, wiping her hands on a dishtowel and hurrying across the room to greet the new arrivals. "We're happy you're here. You probably know everyone—and if not, they know you, Billy, from seeing your face all over town. I swear I've seen more of you in the last six months on posters and the like than since you moved back after college."

Bill laughed along with the others, and made the rounds of hellos. He picked up Phoebe's Emma and lifted her to his shoulders, carrying the delighted toddler around the room.

Janna followed close behind him, carefully greeting everyone. She wore a blue silk jacket and slacks, perfectly tailored and slightly out of place with the casually dressed crowd. Janna seemed slightly ill at ease, Po thought, but that was certainly understandable—she was the new person in a roomful of people who had lived in this small town nearly all their lives. "Janna, come meet the other best two-year-old in the room." She took Janna's hand and led her over to the couch where Phoebe urged her to sit next to her. In minutes Phoebe had plopped one twin on her lap, along with the moose book, and suggested Janna finish it for Jude, who eagerly cuddled up to his new reader.

Janna was a good sport, Po thought. She had clearly been brought up right—gracious, polite, and looked you in the eye when she talked. But beneath it Po sensed that the young, well-bred woman had found out early that her family's wealth couldn't buy everything. She was still puzzled at the match-up between her and Bill, but could see in the way Janna's eyes sought him out that she clearly adored him.

Across the room Gus Schuette was patting Bill on the back, applauding his decision to run for mayor. "You can do it, Billy boy. Bring some new blood to this town."

"The town needs more than blood," Rita cut in. "What do you intend to do for Crestwood, Bill? Give me the facts, not political jibber jabber."

Bill laughed at Rita's forthrightness and answered earnestly. "Well, for starters, I love this town. And I hope to use my father's company as a vehicle for doing some good things. I'm looking into fixing up some old buildings for the town, using some to fill social service needs. I guess that's really why I want to be mayor—so I can give a little back to this town."

"Spoken like a true gentleman. You may have to toughen up a little, Bill, if you want to be a politician," Rita said.

"Oh, I don't know," Bill said. "Maybe Crestwood politics is different and there's room for the likes of me."

Po watched his lopsided smile, his gentle manner, and decided that Bill McKay just might be right. "I remember your father saying you'd be a politician someday," Po said. "He must be proud of this turn in your career."

"We're all proud of Bill," Janna said, looking up from her book. She smiled over at Bill. "Both sets of parents know Bill has nowhere to go but up."

Po watched affection color Janna's face. Bill responded with a nod in her direction and a smile that Po couldn't quite read. She suspected that the attention was making him slightly uncomfortable.

But Bill was good-natured about it. He simply shrugged, offered a half-smile, and joked, "She has me in the White House in five years."

Max Elliott raised a wine glass. "Here, here, to Mayor McKay."

A noisy toast followed, along with well wishes for Bill's campaign and plans. "And now," Po said, "before we propel Billy directly into the White House, I suggest we eat. Pick up a plate from the sideboard before P.J.'s fine steak turns cold."

Friendly laughter nudged the crowd around the table and in minutes plates were heaped full of hot rolls and sweet butter, mounds of basil and corn pasta, and P.J.'s juicy fillets and béarnaise sauce.

Po didn't have a chance to talk to Max Elliott alone until the meal was almost over and empty plates began to stack up on the dining room table. Po walked toward the opposite end of the long room and opened the refrigerator. As she lifted the pies from the freezer, Max appeared at her side.

"Need help, Po?" He set his wine glass on the counter and took the pies from her hands.

"Thanks, Max. Just set those down on the counter." Po pulled a stack of small plates from the counter. "It was nice of you to bring Billy and Janna, Max. I don't think Janna knows many people."

Max nodded. "And doesn't make friends easily, as far as I can tell," he said. "I was meeting with Bill about some company matters, and knew you wouldn't mind if I brought them along."

"Are you helping Bill with his political plans?" Po asked.

"Not so far. Though I'll help him if I can. But I did legal and financial work for the realty company years ago, and Bill has asked me to help him out with a few things to get the company back on track." Max picked up the knife and began slicing through layers of coffee ice cream, thick hot fudge, and a thin, crusty layer of crushed pralines. "Sinful, Po," he moaned, lifting a wide slice and sliding it onto a plate.

"But good for the spirit every once in a while," Po said. She placed a fork on each plate. "Max, I've been wanting to ask you about Picasso—have you spoken to him?"

Max took a drink of his wine, then shook his head.

Po saw the furrows on his brow deepen. He seemed to want to say something to her, but instead, he lifted his wine glass again and drained it.

"Max, what is it?"

Max picked up the tray of pie plates and looked at Po. "The truth is, I wanted to go over to Picasso's as soon as I heard the news. I like Picasso very much. But frankly, Po, I'm not the right person to be with him right now. Make of that what you will."

Before Po could question him further, he walked back to the other end of the room to a chorus of voices welcoming the ice cream pies.

Po watched him as he handed out the plates of dessert, wondering what in the world could cause such uncharacteristic behavior in this gentle man she had come to respect and like very much. It wasn't like Max at all. And she wondered briefly how many other relationships would become awkward because of the murder of a young woman none of them knew.

CHAPTER 9

Sunday night suppers usually ended early so everyone could get home in time to get ready for another week, and tonight's was no exception. Max was the first to go, and Po regretted saying anything to him about Picasso. He seemed troubled when he left, and after a quick kiss on the cheek and thank you, was out the door without another word. The others followed soon after, though Eleanor lingered behind, helping Po put away the last of the dishes.

"Po, you've been distracted tonight. Out with it," Eleanor demanded, pouring the last of the coffee from the pot into her mug.

Po wondered if it was good for Eleanor to have all that caffeine so close to bedtime, but she held her silence, knowing Eleanor would do what she pleased, no matter what anyone said.

"It's Picasso isn't it?" Eleanor said abruptly. "It's awful that he's going through all this."

Po nodded. It was awful, and confusing, and affecting people she cared about. But she knew instinctively that whatever was bothering Max tonight was something she didn't have any right to talk about with others. But the quilt was another matter.

"Eleanor," she said, "something happened today that is plaguing me. I saw a quilt hanging on the wall of Picasso's home." The image of the beautiful bird had remained with Po all evening. She described it to Eleanor in detail, the artful swirl of the fabric pieces, the brilliant colors that made the bird stand out in bold relief. "But the thing that is bothering me, El, the thing that I can't shake, is the almost certain thought that I've seen it before."

"You probably did," Eleanor said, sitting down at Po's wide table, now empty of the platters it held earlier. "Many people make the same quilt, Po, you know that. And from your description, it sounds lovely. Other people have probably used the same pattern."

"It wasn't that kind of quilt, El. It was intricate, unique. I don't think the pattern would have been easily duplicated, and even if it had been, it was the kind of art work that you wouldn't want to pass on to others. But for the life of me, I can't remember where I've seen it."

"Maybe someone did an article on it. Or you saw it at a quilt show. Houston, perhaps? We've certainly been to plenty of shows, and it would explain how you'd seen one from the east coast."

"That's a possibility, Eleanor." Po considered the ideas as she poured herself a cup of tea. She sat down across from Eleanor. "Picasso said he wanted to bring all of us in to see the quilt, but Laurel refused."

"Laurel wasn't the most sociable person in the world, Po. She probably didn't want a bunch of us tramping through her personal space."

"Probably. But it's a shame. Things that beautiful should be shared. But I do wish I could remember exactly where I've seen it before. It will plague me in an awful way."

"It will come to you when you stop thinking about it," Eleanor said philosophically. "Believe me, I'm the expert on memory lapses. And things usually float back. Or not." Tiny lines around her clear blue eyes moved upward as she laughed. "But I will stop by Picasso's house to pay my respects and see it for myself. Now you have me curious, Po Paltrow."

"Good. Maybe between the two of us, we will have a whole memory."

"Or not," Eleanor said, and headed for the door, her cane tapping on the floor as she went.

CHAPTER 10

By Tuesday, Po's thoughts of the bird quilt were buried beneath a cloud of more ugly matters: rumors.

"They're so huge, they could choke a horse," Selma told Po as they scurried across the campus of Canterbury College to attend Leah's evening lecture on women in the 1960s. A brisk breeze had caused the two women to hug their jackets tight to their bodies and keep their step lively. "It seems everyone and her brother has a story to tell about Laurel St. Pierre," Selma muttered, shoving her hands into the pockets of her sweater.

"Kate stopped by this morning on her way to that photography class she's taking. She can barely speak to P.J., she said. She wants him to publicly declare Picasso innocent."

"Maybe he should," Selma said. "Ridiculous thought that such a sweet man would do such a thing."

"Of course it's ridiculous. But with all these rumors spreading, the police need to look at everything."

"That gossipy column in the Gazette claims there's a whole army of men that know Laurel, and not in the way any husband would approve."

"That same column declared improprieties

about Eleanor when she hosted a political dinner the columnist didn't approve of," Po reminded her, nodding toward Eleanor's three-story mansion on the corner of the campus.

Selma laughed. "I remember. Eleanor loved it."

"But you've a point, Selma. Even though the rumors may be nonsense, the fact of the matter is that there's a smidgen of truth mixed in. Laurel did place a domestic violence call just days before she was killed. And when there's a bit of truth involved, rumor and truth become mixed until you can't tell one from the other."

Truth be told, Po was worried sick over Picasso and all the gossip spinning around him. And she knew that the phone call Laurel made to the police wasn't good. It indicated marital trouble, even though Picasso denied it. And he had told Po earlier that day that he was going to reopen the restaurant, just to have something to do. Would people interpret it as a lack of grieving? Po wondered, and thought she might have to talk to Picasso about it, even though she knew that for some, grieving had to be woven into a productive life or it became suffocating and unbearable. But she would tell Picasso to go slow, to take time for himself, too.

Selma held open the door to the Canterbury College auditorium, and the two women walked into the lobby. "Looks like a good crowd," Selma observed. Leah's lectures were popular, and in addition to students and faculty, townspeople often came as well.

"There's Janna Hathaway," Po said, noticing the young woman standing near the window.

Po caught her attention and waved her over. "I'm happy to see you here, Janna—we share an interest in women's history, I guess."

Janna smiled and explained to Po that Bill had a meeting with Max and some others that evening about business matters, and had suggested she come. "He thought it'd be good for me to be aware of things going on in the college community."

Po was disappointed, hoping Janna's motives were personally, rather than politically, motivated, but she quickly swallowed the unkind interpretation of Janna's motives and introduced her to Selma. "Selma has the most amazing fabric in her store that you'll find anywhere, Janna."

"Bill and I will be having some things made for the wedding, Selma. I'll bring my mother's decorator by some day."

"When is the wedding?" Po asked.

"Not for nearly a year. My mother said it will take that long to get everything prepared, though I'd prefer to run off and get married tomorrow."

"Why don't you?" Selma asked. "One of my daughters did that. I was briefly disappointed, I must admit, but she was shy and didn't want all the hoopla. We had a great picnic celebration a few weeks later and everyone was happy."

Janna didn't smile. "That's not the way it works in my family," she said. "One doesn't cross Charles Hathaway."

Janna said her father's name in the way one talked about a foreign dignitary—with distant respect and no warmth—and Po felt an instant of pity for her.

"Come sit with us, Janna," she said, wanting the moment to pass. "Kate may be along as well."

But it wasn't until the question and answer period, following the intriguing lecture on women leaders during the '60s Civil Rights movement, that Kate slid into the seat next to Po. "Sorry, Po," she whispered. "I got caught up in cropping some shots I took today. But there's some I especially want you to have so I brought them along. How about we go for coffee after?"

Coffee ended up being decaf lattes at the college coffee shop. Janna excused herself right after the lecture, but Selma, Kate, Leah, and Po gathered around a corner table and curled their fingers around warm mugs of strong coffee.

Kate pulled a handful of photos out and spread them across the tabletop. "Okay folks, look what I did today."

Po looked at the photos, then quickly picked one up. "It's the quilt. Where did you get these, Kate?"

"I went over to Picasso's and offered to take some shots of it because it's so beautiful. He was pleased, so I enlarged a couple." She looked at Selma and Leah. "I thought Po would like having it because she's trying to remember where she's seen it."

"It's absolutely beautiful," Leah said, holding one of the photos up to the light.

Selma slipped her glasses on, leaned toward Leah, and looked at the photo. "Oh my Lord," she exclaimed, grabbing the photo directly out of Leah's hands and staring at it in disbelief. She looked at Po.

"I know exactly where you've seen this quilt before, Po Paltrow. You've seen it in my shop—a whole lot of years ago. And I'll tell you this much—it wasn't made by Laurel St. Pierre."

CHAPTER 11

Po stared at Selma. Then she took the photo from her and looked at it again. When she finally looked up, her eyes were wide in disbelief. "Esther Woods," she said softly.

"Exactly. I'd know that quilt anywhere. In fact, I talked Esther into letting me display it in the shop during an October quilt competition years ago. That's probably where you saw it, Po."

"Who? What are you talking about?" Kate asked.

"I'm in the dark, too," Leah said. "I never heard of Esther Woods."

"Esther lived in Crestwood before you moved here, Leah," Po said. "And Kate, you probably would never have met her. She lived north of your neighborhood, near the highway, but kept to herself."

"Lived?" Leah asked.

"Esther died years ago," Po said.

"Of a broken heart, if you ask me," Selma said.

"Maybe. But the actual cause was an auto accident. Her husband was driving—"

"Driving drunk, Po. He was drunk as a skunk," Selma said. She took her glasses off and set them on the table.

Po nodded. "Al Woods was a nasty man."

"He drove Esther and himself directly off the bridge just west of town," Selma finished.

"What an awful story," Kate said. She picked up one of the photos and looked again at the beautiful bird caught up in the still-vivid colors of the pieced background design. "But I still don't understand how the quilt got on Picasso's wall. He was quite clear that it belonged to Laurel."

Po shrugged. "I haven't the faintest idea. Unless Eleanor was right and there are copies of this quilt. If Laurel's quilt was the original, maybe Esther had a copy of the pattern and made hers from that."

"No, absolutely not," Selma said. She drained her coffee cup and set it down on the table. Deep wrinkles creased her forehead. "Esther Woods had little in her life that she was proud of. The bird quilt was one of those few things. She designed it, pieced and appliquéd it, and quilted every single stitch herself. I guarantee it."

"So maybe she passed the pattern on to others," Leah said.

Selma shook her head. "No. I don't think she'd have done that. I didn't know Esther well—no one did because Al Woods was so possessive she rarely ventured out. She was a seamstress—worked her little fingers to the bone, so she sometimes came in for thread and other sewing supplies, but not often. But I did know her feelings for her bird quilt, as she called it. She was so proud of it, and when I asked her if I could display it, you'd have thought she'd won the lottery. I think the quilt represented that part of her that was good and whole and happy, and she would never have allowed others to copy it, at least not knowingly. I'd bet my life on it."

"Some people can look at a quilt and figure out the pattern—Susan does that sometimes," Leah said.

"That's true," Selma admitted.

"But look closely at this quilt," Po said, holding a close-up photo of the bird up to the light. "It's so intricate. It's all coming back now. I don't think it could be a copy. I remember the blue and green thread circling around the gold streaks in the bird's wings. And the tiny gold French knots at the tips of the wings."

"Do you suppose Picasso can shed some light on it?" Leah asked, pushing her cup aside, and slipping her arms into the sleeves of her sweater.

"Perhaps," Po said. "We didn't talk about it much the other day."

Leah moved the photos of the quilt around on the table like pieces of a puzzle, seeing it from different angles, admiring the fine design. One picture, slightly stuck beneath the others, came loose, and Leah picked it up.

"What's this, Kate?"

Kate leaned over and looked at the photo. She quickly took it from Leah's hand. "Oh, I didn't mean to include that one." She bit down on her bottom lip and looked from Leah to Po. "I didn't know I had this picture until I downloaded my camera photos onto the computer. I think Amber, one of my students, must have taken it. I met her in the park that day and let her play with the camera for awhile." She paused and stared hard at the photo, her brows pulling together. Her heart had nearly leapt out of her chest when she'd discovered the photo an hour before. It was a clear shot of Laurel St. Pierre in the arms of another man. She'd called P.J. instantly, but his message said he'd be back later, and she remembered, then, a meeting he had told her about. "This is for P.J.," she said aloud. "I'm headed over there on my way home."

"P.J.?" Leah looked more closely at the picture. She frowned. "Is that Laurel?"

"Yes," Kate said. "She was in the park the other day—I think I mentioned it to you, Po. I didn't even know it was Laurel at first. They—Laurel and this man—were standing up near a grove of trees, kind of hidden. When they stepped from the shadow, I realized it was Laurel—and a man. But I didn't know Amber had taken their picture until today."

Po took the picture from Kate's hand and looked at it closely. "The police will want to see this right away, Kate," Po said.

Kate nodded. "That's my plan."

"Oh, my," Selma said. "It's one thing to hear the rumors, but quite another to have a picture of it."

"I almost felt guilty watching them that day," Kate said. "I didn't intend to intrude. But then after Laurel was killed, I told P.J. what I'd seen, but without a description, they couldn't do much except include it in with all the other things people were saying about Laurel."

"But now you have a picture," Leah said. "This is good, Kate."

"Maybe it will help Picasso," Po said.

Kate nodded.

Selma put her glasses back on and looked carefully at the photo. "He looks vaguely familiar. But I can't place him."

The picture was passed around and examined carefully. "Maybe it's someone Laurel knew before they moved here, someone from back east," Leah offered.

"And maybe it's someone who might have a motive for killing her," Kate said.

"From the looks of that photo, that's not what's on his mind." Selma looked at it again, then put it back down on the table.

"Maybe not. But at least it's someone else for the police to concentrate on," Kate said. She scooped up the pictures and stood to slip on her jacket.

The others gathered their purses and coats and pulled out dollar bills to leave on the table for the young waitress waiting to gather their cups.

Kate looked down at the table as if she were still looking at the picture, focusing in on that moment in time. "I was so surprised to see Laurel that day that I kept watching them for a minute. The camera caught the kiss, but there was more that it didn't see. Laurel—and whoever he is— pulled apart right after the embrace. They seemed to be talking briefly, and then the whole lovely scene was shattered by an angry slap. And I think it was Laurel who was doing the slapping."

CHAPTER 12

Wednesdays were writing days for Po, but a restless night left her mind foggy. A run along the river would put her in a better frame of mind, she thought. Perhaps it would bring some writing inspiration and distance her a little from things she couldn't do anything about.

Po was an eclectic writer, having several books of essays to her publishing credit, a book on women and quilting, and occasional articles in magazines. In addition to the article on crazy quilts, her current long-term project was a book of essays on notable Midwestern women, a topic of interest to her, but one clouded over by the week's events.

The morning was brisk, and the air energized Po as she moved along the meandering paths, her slick red jogging pants making swishing noises as she ran. The riverfront park was nearly empty this morning, and Po enjoyed the solitude and time to sift through her tangled thoughts. Kate's pictures of the quilt had unleashed something inside her— a nagging, uncomfortable feeling. And she suspected it would get worse before it got better. She needed to sort through this mess they were mired in, to bring peace back into their days. Esther Woods' bird quilt weighed heavily on her mind. Such a lovely work of art, and sitting there in all its glory on Picasso's wall. But how in heaven's name did it get there? Po suspected Picasso wasn't going to be much help. Only Laurel could tell them, and Laurel certainly wasn't giving any answers.

The river was quiet today as Po ran along its edge. It had been swift, she remembered, the night Laurel had died. She looked across the narrow waterway as she ran, where the path continued but the land behind it was less developed, rugged and craggy with overgrown weeds and thorny bushes. She wondered where Laurel had met someone on that path—and why. The police hadn't said exactly where Laurel had been thrown into the river, only where her body had been found. But it didn't matter much, Po supposed. The path started in the downtown area, and ran all the way past the bridge and for a couple miles south, where a smaller bridge crossed the river and connected the walking path to the one Po ran on now. It could have been any where along the way, and ended in the same grisly way. She shivered as the grim thought of Laurel's murder took hold, and rubbed her arms against the chill. Then she headed up one of the small paths away from the river bank, and back toward the Elderberry Road neighborhood and her own home. As she neared the shops, she slowed down slightly, turned in behind Selma's shop, and began running down the deserted alley. The sight of Picasso's van behind the French Quarter made her smile—any sign of normalcy coming from the grieving Frenchman was a good thing. She ran toward the restaurant, happy to see the kitchen windows open wide and sounds of life coming through the screens. Picasso working was a good thing. She'd have to come in later in the week for his steamed mussels swimming in garlic butter, just the way she loved them. And maybe a small bowl of French onion soup with Picasso's home-baked croutons floating on the top. Now if only she could help dispel the ugly rumors that swirled about his little round head, life would be much better, indeed.

Po slowed to a stop behind the restaurant and breathed in deeply, stretching out one leg and leaning into it, her eyes lifted to the back of the restaurant and the high, kitchen windows on its west corner. Maybe this would be the perfect time to ask Picasso a few more questions about the quilt that hung so stately on his wall. And perhaps he'd offer her a glass of water as well.

As Po brought her body upright, she spotted Picasso's blunt profile just inside the open kitchen window, but before she could call out her hello, he turned away from the window and his voice rose in startling anger. "Vicious man! Judas!" he called out. "You were my friend and you betrayed me!"

Another voice, unfamiliar to Po, murmured an answer. The man must have been standing across the room, and at first his words were indistinct. But before Po had a chance to move away, the man moved closer to the window and his voice rose through it in churlish tones. "I did you a favor, old man," the voice said. "You're better off now, believe it. She was a bitch." The last word was punched out and flew through the window like a hit ball. Po stepped back as if it might hit her directly in her solar plexus.

"Out, get out of my sight!" Picasso yelled. "Don't you ever come back into my restaurant."

"Oh, I'm outta here, all right, and you can shove your business you know where. But it's not over, Frenchy. There's still more I can get out of that scheming wife of yours, and believe you me, I intend to get it!"

Before Po had a chance to move down the alleyway, away from listening in on a private conversation, a broad-shouldered man rushed through the back door, nearly knocking her down. He headed for a sports utility vehicle that had been hidden behind Picasso's van and jumped inside. A shiny black Lab sat upright on the back seat, looking at Po with interest.

Po stared at the man as he jumped into the SUV and brought the engine to life. Only the dog seemed aware of her presence. The man had dark, thick hair, prominent cheekbones, and wide brows marking a strong face. He backed the car recklessly close to the edge of the alley, then lurched into drive and raced down the alley past Po, scattering gravel in all directions. The dog stuck his head out the back window of the car, still looking at Po.

But it was the man, not the dog, that Po recognized. Even in the rush of his departure, Po knew she had seen this person before. There was no doubt in her mind. He was the same man Kate had snapped a picture of—the man who had been standing on the hill kissing Laurel St. Pierre, blown up now into a real-life figure.

CHAPTER 13

Po hesitated only seconds before opening the back door to Picasso's French Quarter restaurant and walking directly into his kitchen.

Picasso was standing at the stainless steel sink, his hands gripping the edge, his head bent low. His breath came in starts and stops.

"Picasso?" Po asked, her voice gentle at the sight of her disturbed friend. "Picasso, who was that man?"

Picasso spun around at the sound of her voice. Thin strands of hair hung limp over his broad forehead. He wore baggy jeans and a stained t-shirt, and his eyes were wild and unfocused.

"Po, what are you doing here?" he managed.

"I apologize for overhearing your conversation, Picasso. I was on my morning run, is all, and I thought I'd stop in for a glass of water. Then I heard voices."

"Water? Yes, yes," Picasso walked over to one of the enormous refrigerators and pulled out a chilled bottle of Evian. He thrust the bottle into Po's hand. "Drink, Po. Sit." He pulled a stool out from beneath the stainless steel island running down the center of the room.

Po thought Picasso was most definitely the one who needed to sit. She pulled out the stool next to hers and motioned toward it. "Let's both sit for a moment. Tell me what is going on, Picasso."

Picasso straddled the stool next to Po and took a deep, heaving breath. When he looked at Po again his eyes were more focused, his face incredibly sad. "Po, Laurel was confused. She was a mixed-up little girl, my Laurelee. People wouldn't understand."

"Laurel was seeing that man?"

He nodded. "His name is Jason Sands. He is my wine distributor. I thought he was a good man. He knows French wines. He travels to France. He loves my crispy frites, my ragout of duck." Picasso clenched his jaw, the sadness that watered his eyes turning suddenly to anger. "But he betrayed me, Po. He used my sweet little wife. He . . ." His fist hit the steel table and the sound rattled through the kitchen.

Po flinched at the force of his movement. It was a side of Picasso she had never seen before, an awful, powerful anger. An anger that, for a brief moment, seemed capable of triggering disastrous actions. Po pushed aside the disturbing thought and focused on the present. "Picasso, listen to me. This is important. Do the police know about Jason Sands?"

Picasso shrugged.

"You must tell them."

"I do not spread family affairs across the whole village, Po. This is a private family matter. What would they think of my Laurel?"

Po bit back a response. Her thoughts about his Laurel had changed considerably in the past few days. She had wounded this man immeasurably, and his love had totally blinded him to it. But Jason Sands was another matter. "Picasso, Jason Sands might be able to tell us something about Laurel's murder. Don't you see?"

"Non. I asked him. He said he didn't do anything to her except tell her he was tired of her. Tired of her! She must have been under a spell. She was working too hard at the restaurant—working so hard and she would never take a penny for it! He took advantage of how tired she was, of her innocence. He used her, Po."

Po took a drink of water and collected her thoughts. Jason Sands may have indeed used Laurel. But there was more to this than Picasso was seeing. Someone needed to talk with the wine distributor. Someone needed to look a lot more carefully into Laurel St. Pierre's quiet life. She worked without pay? Laurel had never impressed Po as one who didn't care about money.

"I know you mean to help me, Po," Picasso said, "and I know people talk about me and make rumors, but I will be fine. You are not to worry."

When Picasso stood and began pulling out knives and vegetables for his special of the day, Po knew it was time to take her leave. Picasso *would* be fine, she suspected. Eventually. But on her short run home, she determined that in the meantime, she'd do all she could to erase the cloud of suspicion that was surely making his life a living hell, no matter what he said.

A shower, fresh jeans, and a nubby red sweater helped Po feel able to face the day. The episode with Jason Sands had stuck to her thoughts like superglue, and she knew that her day was lost until something was done about it. She left a message for P.J., giving him the few scant details that she had, then loaded Hoover into her car for a drive over to Maggie's clinic for a scheduled check-up. Maybe the mundane activity would untangle her thoughts, and she could make some sense out of the morning's encounter.

Maggie's veterinary hospital was in an old house that had been completely renovated into a clinic so friendly that Po never had a problem getting Hoover to his appointments. And the golden retriever loved Maggie Helmers.

"Hey, Hoover, my love, up here," Maggie coaxed, patting the surface of the low examining table. Hoover promptly jumped up and licked her waiting hand while she stepped on a pedal and slowly raised the platform to an examining height.

"So Po, why the frown?" Maggie asked, as her hands deftly examined Hoover's coat.

"Too much activity early in the morning," Po said, and related the events at Picasso's. "I know you're as crazy about that little Frenchman as I am, Maggie. We need to help get rid of this dark aura about him and cast those dangerous rumors to the wind. It will begin to affect his business soon, I'm afraid."

"Do you know any more about the wine distributor? He and Laurel must have been very discreet in meeting one another. This is the first I've heard about it. And believe me, lots of gossip hits these walls between rabies vaccinations and spays."

"Since he was in and out of the restaurant, they probably had plenty of time to plan meetings. And instinct tells me Laurel was a clever woman and could probably hide anything she wanted to from Picasso. Love can blind one very easily."

"Do you think the guy had anything to do with her murder?"

"I think he certainly could be a suspect."

"But why would he kill Laurel?" Maggie gently pressed Hoover's ears wide and checked inside with a tiny light.

"I don't know, Maggie. But Kate said the embrace Amber caught on her camera was followed by a fight of some sort. Perhaps Laurel was breaking up with him?"

"From what you overheard him saying to Picasso, he wouldn't have cared."

"A love scorned may say things like that to save face."

"I suppose that's true. What else do you know about the man?"

"Nothing, really. Except he had a beautiful black Labrador sitting in his back seat."

Maggie perked up at the mention of one of her favorite breeds. Her tendency to identify people by their pets was well-known among her friends. "Black Lab? What did you say his name was?"

"Sands, I think. He had a Kansas license plate, so I guess he lives around here somewhere."

"Sands . . ." Maggie pondered the name as she lowered the examining table and allowed Hoover off to sit on the floor next to Po. "Was he a big guy?"

"I'd say so. A little rough looking."

Maggie turned toward her computer and tapped a few keys, then squinted and scrolled down through a list of names. "Sands . . . Albert Einstein. Five-year-old Labrador Retriever. Bingo, Po. They're clients!"

CHAPTER 14

According to Maggie's records, Jason Sands lived with his dog, Albert Einstein, just outside the city limits of Crestwood, not far from the wooded estate that Susan shared with her elderly mother. Which was the reason Po used to convince herself to drive out that way. She needed to pick up some books from Susan, and today was as good a time as any. With Hoover in the back seat, Po headed west.

Nothing in Crestwood was very far away from anything else, and it took Po less than fifteen minutes to spot the winding road that led to Jason Sands' home. She had intended to drive on by, but curiosity forced the car right onto Hilltop Lane, and before she realized it, she was driving slowly down the street. Po had no idea what she'd do when she passed the house, but curiosity propelled her to at least see where this man—now a piece in the growing puzzle of Laurel's murder—lived.

The country road was dotted with new, ranch-type homes. Several houses were under construction, indicating the area would soon be absorbed into the city, but for now, it still held the flavor of country. The same address that Maggie had scribbled on a piece of paper for Po was posted on the mailbox in front of one of the few older homes on the road. It was a small one-story house, bordered by a split-rail fence and with a large yard that stretched back to the woods behind it. A good place for Albert Einstein to play, Po thought. Not to mention that the remote area would have been a good place to shield an affair. The black SUV she had seen at Picasso's earlier was nowhere to be seen. Po drove past the house and turned around at the end of the road, then headed back down the street toward the main road. She wasn't sure, really, why she had even come. It would be foolish for her to stop and talk to this stranger. Maybe even dangerous. And what would she say, even if she did stop? But somehow she felt a need to situate Jason Sands somewhere, before she shared his relationship with Laurel with P.J. and the police. Maggie had only vague recollections about the man, except that he had flirted with her receptionist and had made an off-color remark when Albert was in for his rabies vaccination. She knew everything there was to know about Albert Einstein, though, and reported that he was well cared for and a lovely dog. "Albert is a regular here for wellness exams. He's been a patient for a year or so," she'd said.

As Po headed back past the house, she noticed Albert flying around the side of the house, chasing a yellow ball. As she slowed the car, a figure emerged from beyond the trees, calling to the dog. But it wasn't Jason Sands. It was a young woman, dressed in jeans and a large sweatshirt.

Not wanting to be noticed, Po picked up speed and continued down the street, glancing in her rearview mirror as she neared the highway. The woman was leaning over, tugging the ball from the dog's mouth. As she straightened up and her sweatshirt flattened out against her body, Po noticed something else—Albert Einstein's playmate appeared to be at least six months pregnant.

"Po, you shouldn't be getting involved in this. You and Kate are messing with serious stuff here," said P.J. He and Po sat on her back porch, drinking chilled martinis, a ritual Po and Kate's mother Liz had begun many years before when their kids were young and their days overflowed with kids' activities with little time left for themselves.

"P.J., I'm not messing with anything. I am reporting this to you as any good citizen would."

"And your goddaughter reported it, too, bursting in on a meeting I had last night. She had that blurry picture clutched in her hand as if the murderer was now signed, sealed, and delivered."

"It wasn't blurry. You could see the man's face when she enlarged it. It *was* Jason Sands, P.J."

"Okay, maybe it was. I was having a drink with Bill McKay and Max when Kate tracked me down. We all looked at the photo when Kate thrust it in our faces. Kate has decided to get the whole town involved in protecting her buddy."

"Bill McKay and Max Elliott aren't the whole town, P.J. But they both do know a lot of people—Billy with his campaigning and Max knows everyone. Did they know him?"

"Don't think so. I thought at first Billy did, but when he looked closer, he said the picture was too fuzzy." P.J. laughed. "Kate was very offended at that. I thought she was going to whack Billy with her backpack. She's a wild woman, Po, when she sinks her teeth into something. Billy did pick up on Kate's idea that Laurel was having an affair, though. Thought that was a distinct possibility."

"Why? Did he know Laurel?"

"Nope. But when you're in politics, I guess you get to know human nature, what makes people do what."

"What did Max think?"

"Max didn't offer any opinion. He clams up when the murder topic comes up. If I didn't trust the guy with my life, I'd think he knew more than he was saying." P.J. took a sip of his martini.

Po refrained from agreeing with him aloud, and instead, sipped her martini and watched the expression on P.J.'s face when he talked about Kate. She knew, too, that Kate could be exasperating—and she reacted to it exactly like P.J. did—with great affection.

"So what now?" Po asked.

"Well, believe it or not, Po, the guys working this case aren't out to get Picasso without doing their homework. They already knew about the affair, you'll be happy to know, though they didn't know it was with Sands. You can be sure they'll look into it and bring the guy in for questioning."

"So they'll let up on Picasso?"

P.J. paused for a moment and took a sip of his martini, then shook his head. "No, Po, they won't let up on Picasso. He doesn't have an alibi and there was documented evidence of problems in the marriage. They can't dismiss that until something else shows up."

"But, P.J., you know and I know that he is innocent."

P.J. didn't answer. He lifted his martini glass and drained the last drops of cocktail, then stared out into the evening darkness that was falling heavily onto Po's wooded yard. The trees were ghostly shapes, the brick pathways lost in shadow. The only movement was the slow gait of Hoover as he padded around the yard, patrolling his empire.

Po didn't look at P.J., but she felt a sadness spread across the porch. She sensed P.J.'s uncertainty, and she read in his silence what she already knew—that finding out more about Laurel and Picasso St. Pierre may not be all that it was cracked up to be. The answers they sought might be far from the ones they wanted to find.

CHAPTER 15

When the Queen Bees arrived at Selma's Saturday morning to work on Picasso's quilt, the air was filled with more than flying fingers and the whirr of the sewing machine. Picasso St. Pierre was on everyone's mind.

"Okay, what can we do, ladies?" Phoebe asked. Her short golden mop was growing out slightly, and she looked more angelic, Eleanor told her, less of an imp. "But that only means you can't judge a book by its cover," Eleanor had added with a wink. As the oldest and the youngest members of the quilting group, Phoebe and Eleanor had forged an unusual bond, and their affection for one another was mirrored in gentle teasing.

"Here's what I say we do, Phoebe," Eleanor answered her now. "We rally together, put our noses to the ground like bloodhounds, and don't let one single rumor fly by us without tracking down its source. These tales are revolting, if I do say so myself. And the fact that Picasso is defending himself about as vigorously as a newborn is, quite frankly, damn stupid."

"At least newborns shriek," Phoebe said, with the conviction of one-who-knows.

"Picasso came to a meeting of the shop owners last night," Selma said. "And that was a good thing, I think. He needs to be around people, needs people to see that he's still the same Picasso, one who couldn't harm a flea." She glanced at the large round clock on the wall, then rose and walked toward the archway that separated the back workroom of her shop from the front of the store. "Back in a minute so don't say anything of interest 'til I come back. I promised Janna Hathaway I'd show her some designer fabrics for that new home she and Bill McKay are building."

"We'll fill you in," Po said. "And if Janna wants to see a quilt in progress, invite her back for coffee. I don't think she knows many people in town yet."

As Selma disappeared into the front of the store, Eleanor pulled the conversation back to her concern about the restaurateur. "I could shake Picasso. He is so self-absorbed and determined to enshrine Laurel as a saint that he doesn't give a hoot what's happening around him."

"It's only been a week," Po said, pulling out several thin strands of gold fabric that she had cut out to represent the bouillabaisse's saffron flavoring. Although she agreed entirely with everything Eleanor said, she knew first-hand the erratic pattern of grieving, and Picasso hadn't even had a chance to start yet. She wondered if she would have had the strength—or even the desire—to protect herself if any ill talk had surrounded Sam's death several years ago.

"Po's right," Kate said. "We need to fill in and do what Picasso can't do. And right now that means defending him. I don't think the police are convinced at all that he's innocent of Laurel's death."

"That's because they don't have anyone else to blame, no other clues except for the wine guy," Maggie said. She was sitting at the end of the table, her fabric for the background blocks laid out in front of her. "And speaking of the wine guy, there's a suspect if ever I saw one. Don't you think so, Po?"

"I certainly think he deserves some attention." She looked up from her sewing. "After we talked, Maggie, I drove by his house. I was probably being snoopy, but it was right on the way to Susan's and somehow the car just turned that way." She told the group about seeing the familiar black Lab—and then the pregnant woman who appeared in the yard.

"This fellow lives near me?" Susan asked.

"On the other side of the woods," Po said. "A world away from your lovely home."

"So he has a pregnant wife," Phoebe said. "And he was having an affair with Laurel, who was probably putting the screws to him. If that's not motive, tell me what is?" Phoebe shoved back her chair and walked over to the long table running under the back windows. Today it held the coffee pot and a crumb cake from Marla's bakery. The cake was still warm and tiny flakes fell from her fingers as she lifted it to her mouth.

"P.J. said they were going to question him," Po said.

"I asked P.J. last night what the guy had to say for himself, and he said they haven't been able to find him," Kate said. "The police don't seem too concerned. Picasso is still their main suspect."

"Oh, that's great. I think sometimes the police can't see the forest for the trees. No offense, Kate," Maggie said.

"No offense taken. You can lump P.J. right in the middle of that description. Why is it that men can't acknowledge the power of emotion and intuition? We all know Picasso is innocent. Facts . . . that's all they think about."

"So we'll give them facts," Leah said. She picked up a subtly patterned piece of fabric and held it up to the light. It was coral-colored, and would be blended with other warm colors—all the way to a velvety chocolate-brown—and used to form small pockets for the scales of her brilliant fish. "And I think the place we should start is with Laurel herself, not with Picasso."

"I've been thinking the same thing," Po said. "Laurel is a mystery, and I don't think we'll be able to budge on this until we figure out exactly who this woman was."

"That's easy to say," said Phoebe. "But she only

lived here a year. She kept to herself. How do we even begin?"

"Esther's quilt," Po, Leah, and Kate said in unison. The collision of their voices startled the others, and Po began to laugh. "I guess at least half of us agree on that point," she said.

Phoebe looked down at the pieces of fabric spread across the table. Picasso's quilt was actually taking shape. Susan had finished pinning the two magnificent fish onto Eleanor's background blocks to get a look at the blend of color and shape, and she moved Po's blocks beneath it.

"Okay, I give," she said. "How in blazes is this quilt going to tell us a thing about Laurel St. Pierre? And who's Esther?"

"No, not *that* quilt, Phoebs, this one." Kate pulled the pictures of Esther Wood's quilt out of her backpack and lined them up on the table.

Selma walked back in with Janna in tow and spotted the photographs. "Esther's quilt," she said, walking over to the table and nearly forgetting her quest.

"Hi Janna," Kate said. "I think you know everyone. Have a seat." She patted the empty chair next to her. "We really do work on quilts back here, but at this moment we're trying to figure out a puzzling thing—a quilt that was made here in Crestwood years ago, then ended up back here under mysterious circumstances."

As Po walked over to the coffee pot, she

watched Janna try to make sense of Kate's explanation. She was glad Selma brought Janna back to the workroom. The Queen Bees could certainly introduce her around and make her feel more at home in the town that would soon be her home. Po handed Janna a mug of coffee and a small plate of crumb cake. "Selma, tell the others what you know about the quilt," Po urged. "It's certainly an odd coincidence, finding it on Laurel's wall."

When Selma finished her story, Phoebe planted her small fists into her hips and said, "Well that's that, then. We start right here to find out about Laurel St. Pierre." She thrust her finger down on one of the photos.

"With a woman who's been dead for fifteen years?" Susan asked.

"Yes," Po answered for Phoebe. "That's exactly where we start. It's the only thing we know about Laurel, other than she lived on the east coast and was poor and drab when she met Picasso. So let's start with the quilt and try to figure out how Laurel got it. Picasso's not much help. All we know from him is that the quilt was her most prized possession. She treated it like a child, taking it down from the wall, dusting it, repairing little loose ends."

"Maybe she just liked quilts and bought it somewhere?" Janna offered. Phoebe stopped talking, startled at the first words to come from their quiet guest's mouth. They had almost forgotten she was there.

"But how did she get it?" Kate asked. "That's the real mystery here. How did Esther's quilt get to the east coast?"

"Maybe Laurel got it around here, at some auction or flea market. I've found some of my favorite fat lady art that way," Maggie said. Maggie's collection of fat lady art had grown over the past couple of years, and included more than twenty pieces. The Bees all added to it whenever they came across statues or postcards or paintings, and the beauty of the Rubenesque figures enchanted them all.

"Or E-bay. There are hundreds of quilts on E-bay," Eleanor said. "My cousin Madeline is addicted. Buys one a week."

"But Picasso says the quilt's been with her since he's known her," Kate said. "That may predate E-bay's popularity."

"I knew so little about Esther Woods," Selma said, "other than her quilting talent. And that she was married to the poorest excuse for a man that I've ever seen."

While the gathering around the table continued to pick away at the mystery of Esther's quilt, Susan and Leah carefully pinned some partially sewn sections of appliqué to a corkboard on the wall.

Po watched them out of the corner of her eye while keeping one ear to the conversation swirling around the table. "It's going to be beautiful!" she said, breaking away from the conversation. "Picasso will be so pleased."

Susan and Leah stepped back and looked at their handiwork. They had sewn the body of the two fish above Po's blocks, which were taking shape in a design of subtly patterned fabric triangles in all different shades of black and silver and deep, shiny gray. The blend of colors and placement of the triangles made the pot appear round on the edges, a perfect boiling cauldron for the colorful fish.

"The colors will go well with the rustic look of the bistro," Eleanor said. "It's quite perfect."

"How nice of all of you to do this for him," Janna said.

"He's a friend," Po answered simply. Janna seemed surprised at the friendship bonds, and Po was determined to see that she felt the strength of those bonds, too.

"I've an idea I want to run by all of you," Selma said, standing beside the quilt pieces pinned to the wall. "Next Friday I'm having a display of appliqué quilts for the first Friday event, and I thought I might use Picasso's quilt to show a work in progress."

"Great idea!" Phoebe said, helping herself to the last piece of crumb cake. The others echoed her support, and Susan offered to figure out how to display it.

During the school year, weekends brought many visitors to Crestwood for Canterbury College events, and the Elderberry shop owners had taken to scheduling special events each first Friday of the month. The stores offered special sales, displays, and sometimes lectures or demonstrations. Selma's quilt displays were a big draw and brought many parents and alumni to the Elderberry shops. In nice weather, especially, the crowds were considerable and flowed onto the small patio areas beside the Brew and Brie and along the street.

"This is good timing," Po said. "First Fridays are festive, and Elderberry Road could use a little festivity right now."

"Agreed," Maggie said, settling down next to the sewing machine at the end of the table. "And I for one, will have—"

A rattle at the back door stopped Maggie's words mid-sentence, and before anyone could get up to open it, Picasso burst into the room. The first thing Po noticed was that he was dressed much better today, his jeans freshly laundered and his apron clean. But the look on his face was anything but ordinary.

"Picasso," she said, "what is it? You look like you've seen a ghost."

"No, not a ghost, Po."

Kate moved quickly to his side, afraid he was going to topple over in front of them. She

120

reached out and took his arm, steadying him. "Picasso, what is it?" She looked into his troubled eyes and detected a trace of fear.

"The police—they found Jason Sands."

"That's good, Picasso. Good news," Po said. "Maybe Mr. Sands can shed some light on all this."

Picasso shook his head. "No, Po. They found him in a quarry. Shot. Jason Sands is dead."

CHAPTER 16

News of Jason Sands' death spread through the small town like a Prairie dust storm. Although not many people knew the traveling wine distributor, his link to Laurel St. Pierre was delicious fodder for the Crestwood gossip mill.

Kate walked into Gus's bookstore later that day and knew without asking that the small group gathered around the check-out counter was dissecting the latest event.

"H'lo Kate." Gus Schuette stepped away from the cluster of customers and greeted her. "What can I do you for?"

"Some good news, Gus. That's what I'm looking for. Good news and something to make me laugh."

"Ah, Katie, girl, it'll work out. Don't fret." Gus Schuette had watched Kate Simpson grow from a mischievous rug rat curled up on his floor reading kids' books to the tall beauty with the high cheekbones standing in front of him. The one thing about Kate that hadn't changed a bit was her irreverent laughter and her broad smile. Today both were noticeably absent. "Looking for that long stalk of wheat?"

Kate nodded. "He was supposed to meet me here. He's late."

"Nope. Beat you to it. He's back in the history and mystery section, wouldn't you know?"

Gus's bookstore was one of Kate's favorite hangouts in all of Crestwood. The maze of rooms, jam-packed with old and new books, the soft strains of Vivaldi in the background, and the smell of thick, dark coffee from the old percolator in the corner brought comfort to her soul. She smiled at Gus, gave him a quick tap on the shoulder, and walked toward the long wide room in the back of the store.

Kate scanned the room. Late-afternoon sunshine poured down on the old, pock-marked library table that centered the room. Reading chairs were tucked into corners between the tall bookshelves. An old man Kate recognized from her neighborhood snoozed in a corner chair, a cup of coffee on the floor at his side and a tattered Ed Bain mystery moving up and down on his chest as he slept.

Kate walked along the parallel stacks, looking down each row. At the end of the last aisle she spotted P.J., squatting on the floor with a stack of books in front of him. "Hi good lookin'," she said, walking toward him.

P.J. uncurled his long frame and stood up. "Not mad at me anymore?" He smiled slightly.

"Not this instant. Give it awhile."

P.J. put his books back on the shelf and wrapped an arm around her shoulder, guiding her back toward the table. "How did the ladies take the latest bombshell?"

"Not happily. We thought Sands was a likely suspect and would take some of the pressure off Picasso. Sands had motive, especially after Po spotted the pregnant wife outside his house."

"Not a wife, apparently. Just another girl-friend. The guy was a regular lothario."

"His only redeeming quality so far is Albert Einstein."

P.J. nodded. "That's about right. But it sure doesn't help Picasso."

"Po took him home. He was pretty shaken."

"It doesn't look good for him, Kate. Sands was meeting someone, apparently, when he was shot. Picasso's number was recorded on his cell phone."

"That doesn't mean anything, P.J. Picasso did business with the guy. He could have called him about wine or something."

"Or something," P.J. repeated. "The girlfriend said Sands was real happy the past few days.

Told her they might even get married and move to a bigger house somewhere. He was 'in the money' he told her."

"But why would Picasso give money to a man he hated?"

"Maybe he knew something about Picasso. Maybe Laurel told him things."

"Or maybe she told him things about some-one else, P.J." Kate pushed a strand of hair behind her ear and started walking toward the front of the store. "Laurel certainly holds all the answers right now. Whoever she is."

"What does that mean?" P.J. walked quickly to catch up with her, watching her pluck three paperback mysteries off the shelves as she went.

"I think there's plenty about her we don't know, P.J.," Kate said over her shoulder. "She's been here a whole year and no one knows her. Even Janna Hathaway is making friends here—she's only been around a short while and she's as shy as a teenager on her first date. People don't let people remain strangers in Crestwood. But Laurel did. Why?"

"She had Picasso and the restaurant. She was certainly no stranger to Jason Sands. And that young waiter at the restaurant is clearly smitten with her. Just because she didn't have women friends doesn't mean she was alone."

Kate looked at him. "Okay, I'll give you that. But what do we know about her? About where she came from? Why did she and Picasso move here, of all places? Didn't she have any friends anywhere who can tell us about her? Relatives? Isn't it a bit odd that she seems to have dropped out of nowhere?"

P.J. watched the animation travel through Kate's body, painting her high cheekbones the color of dewy roses, spreading out into her arms until they moved from the sides of her body and swept the air in large curves. Her head moved with her words, and her spirit lit a small fire right in the pit of his stomach. She wore a long-sleeved blue sweater and a pair of gray pants, and, to P.J., she was nearly queenly in the simple outfit. "Good questions, Kate," he managed to say in carefully modulated tones. "And believe it or not, we're asking some of those questions ourselves down at the station."

"Well, I should hope so." Kate dropped her books on the front counter and smiled at Gus. "Could you please put them on my tab, Gus?"

Gus grumbled a response, feigning displeasure, and pulled out a scrap of paper for her to sign. He didn't do it for just anyone. But long-time customers could still count on Gus to send them a bill. Hell, if he couldn't trust Kate Simpson, who could he trust?

"Don't trust her, Gus. She owes me a fiver."

"He's a liar, Gus," Kate said.

And then Gus was treated to the laugh he'd

125

missed with all the dire goings-on. It was well worth the cost of three used Dorothy Sayers mysteries.

Kate gathered up her books and turned to P.J. "Now feed me," she said, "or I'll have to find someone who will."

Even in Crestwood, restaurants on Saturday nights usually had a wait. P.J. and Kate picked Picasso's, partly because it was close, but mostly because they knew that, though he had faithful clientele, the numbers had fallen off this week, and he would welcome the business.

Kate and P.J. walked across the small patio separating Gus's store from Picasso's and looked through the open door. Several tables were filled, but there wasn't the usual pile-up at the door with folks sitting on the benches waiting for their name to be called.

"Come in," said Picasso, when he spotted them at the door. He moved quickly toward them and spread his arms wide, embracing Kate and P.J. in one giant hug.

Kate pulled back and looked closely at him. His smile seemed forced. "Picasso, has anything happened?"

Picasso pressed a finger to her lips. "Shhh, my sweet Kate. Everything will be fine."

A vibration from his cell phone caused P.J. to excuse himself. He stepped aside to take the call.

"You're sure you don't want to tell me?" Kate asked. Picasso certainly had reason to be upset, but Kate knew him well enough now to know Picasso had an unusual knack for pouring himself into the present. And tonight, he was somewhere else.

P.J. walked back over and looked at Picasso. "Were you going to tell us, Picasso?"

Kate's heart skipped a beat. "Tell us what?"

"It is nothing. Someone—maybe a vagrant—came into my house this morning while I am here at the restaurant, and—"

"What?" Kate stepped closer and tried to keep her voice down.

P.J. put a hand on her arm. "According to the guys who checked on it—and Picasso concurs—nothing was taken. Not a thing. The lock was broken, that's about it." He looked over at Picasso. "Have you considered an alarm system?"

"Non! We never had such things in my village. How would friends get in if you were not at home?"

"Or enemies," P.J. muttered.

"It is all right. Nothing is gone. Nothing. We forget it now. You are here, and friendly faces are tonic for my soul."

Picasso ushered them inside and brushed away any more mention of the break-in, forbidding them to discuss it.

"And see who else comes to my bistro for the

very first time? Our future mayor." Picasso linked his arm in Kate's and led them over to a table by the bar where Bill McKay and Janna Hathaway sat with a bubbling hot plate of escargots between them.

"Hey, Kate and P.J.," Bill said, standing and greeting them. "How about joining us?"

"Ah, of course," Picasso said. "Four lovely young people, enjoying my magnificent food. Sit, sit." He pulled out a chair for Kate. "I finally got this young man to come into my restaurant."

"You're sure we're not interrupting an intimate dinner for two?" Kate asked.

"We love the company," Janna said politely. "Would you like some wine?"

Andy Haynes appeared as if by magic and set two more places. Kate noticed the sadness on his face and realized how he must be missing Laurel, too. Picasso wasn't the only one whose lives she had touched—for good or for bad.

After a brief consultation with Picasso, the diners all followed his recommendation and ordered the paper-wrapped Chilean sea bass, "light, subtle, and flavorful," he said with great conviction, "with a perfectly seasoned medley of fresh vegetables."

"So, Kate," Bill said when wine was poured, a warm baguette brought to the table, and another platter of escargots passed around. "Looks like your fuzzy picture nailed the right guy."

"Fuzzy my foot," Kate said, pretending to be insulted.

"I concede," Bill said, tipping his head slightly.

"So how are things with the case, P.J.?" Bill asked.

"Oh, so-so," P.J. said.

"Right," Kate broke in, "two unsolved murders, frightened townsfolk, innocent suspects—just your usual day at the office." She didn't mention the break-in, honoring Picasso's request. And perhaps he was right, it could have been a homeless person looking for some food. Picasso's home would certainly be a good choice.

"Don't mind Kate," P.J. said. "She likes things done yesterday."

"Do you have any leads?" Janna asked.

"We're gathering information. Things are moving along."

"I heard the wine distributor had lots of folks who might like to see him gone," Bill offered. "A girl-in-every-port kind of guy."

"I think the person we need to concentrate on is Laurel and who she was," Kate said. She kept her voice low and looked over now and then to be sure they wouldn't upset Picasso with their talk.

"What do you mean?" Bill asked.

"No one seems to know anything about her, where she came from. Yet she had a quilt in her home that was made by someone right here in Crestwood."

"Is that important?" Bill said. "Why couldn't she have a quilt made by someone in Crestwood?"

"Well, she could. She *did,*" Kate said, impatient with his misunderstanding. "Laurel had a beautiful quilt that she cherished. She had it for years, long before she and Picasso moved here from the east coast—and it was made by a woman here in town."

"Who?" Bill asked.

"Esther Woods," Kate said. "Did you know the Woodses? Your parents lived here forever," Kate asked.

Bill took a drink of wine and considered the name, then shook his head. "I don't think so. It's a common name, though. But about the quilt, aren't they like other art pieces? They could certainly be purchased and moved around the country."

"Bill's right," Janna said. "My mother's decorator attends auctions all over the country."

"I don't think that's what happened," Kate said. She paused to mop up the buttery escargot sauce with a piece of bread. "There's a connection here between that quilt, and Laurel, and, well, and something we haven't figured out yet." She looked longingly at her butter-sopped fingers, wondering if Janna's fine breeding would think it awful if she licked them.

"And maybe Kate will actually let the police

find out what the connection is, *if* there's a connection." P.J. took a drink of his wine, watching Kate over the top of the glass.

Kate ignored him and turned toward Janna. "I don't know if you detected our sleuthing skills this morning, Janna, but the Queen Bees are pretty good at it."

"Kate," P.J. warned.

Kate held up her hands. "P.J., I know this is your job, not mine. And I know you're better at it. But I also know that the longer this drags out, the more frightened people become."

"And you also know it's dangerous as hell to be stalking a murderer," P.J. said, putting down his napkin.

Kate noticed the sharp tone to P.J.'s voice and realized that in her fervor she had pushed him an inch too far. She smiled sweetly into his frown, touched his shoulder affectionately, and said, " 'Nuf said, Flanigan. Consider me put in my place."

"That'll be the day," P.J. said.

"How about some happy talk, like football?" Bill said, trying to salvage the peace.

"Football?" Kate grimaced.

"Gus Schuette showed me some old clippings today," Janna explained. "And there was one of P.J."

"P.J.?" Kate said.

"My senior year," Bill said. "He saved the homecoming game with Lawrence. Intercepted a

131

pass and carried it all the way down the field for a TD."

P.J. laughed. "My moment of glory," he said.

"I remember!" Kate said. "You were a hero."

"Gus also told me Bill was captain," Janna said proudly.

"Oh, he probably was," Kate said, laughing. "And probably threw a zillion passes that day."

"But credit where it's due," Bill said. "That was definitely P.J.'s game."

P.J. was actually blushing, Kate thought. And how nice of Bill to bring up P.J.'s great game. Bill was usually the quarterback hero, she remembered, and it was nice of him to pass the glory around. She grinned at P.J. and rose to go to the ladies' room, smiling a thank-you to Bill for salvaging P.J.'s mood and getting her out of a mess of trouble.

P.J. grabbed her fingers and whispered, "Come back soon." His tone was softer and Kate felt his smile on her back as she walked away from the table.

Kate walked down the narrow hallway to the restrooms and noticed Andy Haynes standing by the kitchen door. "Hi, Andy," she said. "How're you doing?"

"Not great, Kate."

"You miss Laurel."

"Yeah. Hey, I know she was playing with me, but there was something about her, something that just got to me, you know?"

"I think I do, Andy. I had that feeling about my high school math teacher. Then he gave me a C and it was all over."

Andy managed a small smile.

"Did you and Laurel talk a lot?" Kate leaned up against the wall next to Andy.

"Yeah, we did. She really listened to me. And she told me things that bothered her, too."

"Like what?"

"Like this town. She didn't like it here much. She was going to leave."

"Why?" Kate felt a twinge of guilt for pummeling Andy for information, especially after the uncomfortable moment with P.J., but talking to someone she used to baby-sit for surely couldn't be dangerous.

"I dunno. She said the town was evil or something. Said bad things happened here. And as soon as she was done, she was leaving."

"Done with what?"

Andy shrugged. "Laurel didn't always make sense. Like sometimes she talked about really nice people—like Mr. Elliott for instance—like they were bad or something."

"She didn't like Max Elliott?

"Hated him. She wanted me to be mean to him, too. But I liked him enough, I guess."

Kate frowned. What an odd person to hate. Everyone liked Max.

"And she had bad headaches, Kate. Real bad.

Sometimes when we were in the kitchen, she'd ask me to rub her shoulders—it helped make her feel better."

"You were good to her, Andy."

"But it wasn't me she was leaving with. I would have though. I'd have taken her anywhere."

"But she had Picasso."

Andy shook his head. "No, that Sands guy. I told her he was no good. I'd see 'em in the kitchen together, laughing. He'd touch her, you know. She thought he would take her away. He was a bad guy, Kate."

Andy's young face turned hard as stone and Kate reached out and touched his arm.

"But he didn't deserve to die, Andy."

Andy pulled away from her touch. "He was bad, Kate."

Kate watched the emotion sweep across his face. It was a very adult distress for such a young guy. Poor kid, she thought. He had fallen hard. And it would be a long while before Laurel St. Pierre released her hold on him, even in death.

When Kate returned to the table, the restaurant was emptying out, and Picasso had pulled up a chair to their table and was talking intently to Bill, Janna, and P.J., his elbows pressed against the white tablecloth.

"She loved it like a child," Kate heard him say, and she realized with a start he was talking about the quilt again, sharing it so intimately with almost strangers. *He must have such a need to talk,* she thought, and slipped quietly into her chair.

Bill was listening carefully to Picasso, his handsome face filled with compassion. "Blankets seem to hold an important place in people's lives," he offered quietly.

"Oh, mon ami, it was so much more. Laurel soothed it, rubbed it, pulled its little seams apart, slipped her lovely hands inside the quilt's folds, then patted it so gently and sewed the seams back together again, like a mother bandaging her little one. I think it held the secrets to her life, that quilt."

Kate watched the exchange and thought again what a good listener Bill was. Janna had shifted slightly in her chair and seemed to be more interested in watching the bus boys' antics near the kitchen door, and P.J., while half-listening, was miles away, probably planning new ways to approach the mystery of Laurel St. Pierre.

And off in the corner she spotted Andy Haynes, his face masked in a terrible mixture of anger and grief. Kate felt tiny goosebumps lift on her arms. She stared at Andy's eyes, and in that horrifying moment, she realized that the love Andy harbored for Laurel St. Pierre was beyond reason, beyond the norms of behavior. And for a brief moment, she wondered what such a love could cause a young man to do.

CHAPTER 17

Sometimes information came from odd places and arrived when you were least expecting it, Kate discovered. It was a chance encounter with her elderly neighbor two days later that sent her rushing off to Po's early Monday morning.

Danny Halloran and his wife Ella had lived next door to the Simpsons since long before Kate was born. They had been old since Kate could remember, but nothing about them ever seemed to change much, not the shuffle of old Danny's walk, not the pudgy, ornery face of Ella, with her thin gray hair pulled back into a knot at the base of her wide neck. They'd lived in their house, Danny used to tell her, when all the land around was prairie, and you could see nearly all the way to Kansas City. Though Kate had learned early to only believe half of what Danny said, she loved his tales.

Danny was a well-liked eccentric among the neighborhood kids, always wanting to know what they were doing and what was up in their world. Ella was not so friendly, her plump face pulled into a perpetual frown. But she had a good soul underneath, Kate's mother repeatedly told her, ever fearful that Ella's cranky disposition would make her the object of kids' neighborhood pranks.

"So what's up, Katie girl?" Danny asked as they met at the end of their driveways to pick up the Monday morning paper. "Anything new about that Frenchman's wife?"

"Nope, Danny, no news." Kate picked up Danny's paper and handed it to him, then picked up her own. She had just jumped out of the shower and her thick, damp hair curled loosely around her cheeks. "But who knows, maybe there'll be some tidbits in today's paper."

"I heard about the quilt that she had hanging on her wall, Esther Woods' quilt. Ella heard it on the morning news today."

Kate hid her surprise. How did that make the news so soon, she wondered? But probably the police had checked it out, took pictures, maybe, of Picasso's house. "Yeah, go figure."

"She was Ella's friend, you know."

"Esther Woods was Ella's friend?" Kate stopped in her tracks and stared at Danny.

"Well, maybe not friend. Ella's not big on friends, don't you know, but Esther Woods used to make clothes for her a while back. That was when Ella got out more, you know, and before the Woods lady died."

"So Ella went to her home?"

"Yep, now and again. I drove her over myself. Small little place, not far from the railroad tracks."

"Did Ella know Esther's husband?"

"Saw him once or twice, I think. Anyone who ever set foot in a Crestwood tavern knew Al Woods—he hit 'em all. Awful man. Even my Ella thought it a crime for Esther to stay with him, and she used to tell her as much. But she had no place to go and needed a roof over her and the child's head."

"The Woodses had a child?" Kate helped Danny up the steps to his house. It was getting more and more difficult for him to climb, and Kate suspected that he and Ella would have to find an assisted living place soon.

"Yep, they did. Poor kid. Always looked like someone had just stolen her puppy dog, if you know what I mean. It was a good thing when Esther finally sent her away. Got her out of the house, away from that man."

"Esther Woods sent her daughter away?"

"Seems so. Can't remember the details exactly." He squinted, looking back into his mind for the facts. "Nope, it was a curious thing—she was there one day when I took Ella for her fitting, and then she was gone. Poof!" He snapped his fingers in the air, then grasped the side of the railing and sucked in a deep lungful of air. "Whew, these steps get higher every day, Katie."

"You better go in and rest, Danny." Kate's mind was spinning, but she wanted Danny safe in a chair before she took off. "I'll check on you later."

Danny let the door slam shut behind him, and Katie watched through the screen while he settled into his worn recliner. Then she spun around on her clunky sandals, ran inside her house for the keys to her Jeep, and headed for Po's.

As Kate drove down Elderberry Road, she noticed Po walking toward Selma's.

Po saw Kate and waved, then frowned in exasperation as Kate made a quick U-turn in the middle of the road and pulled into a parking spot in front of Max Elliott's law office. She jumped out of the car and ran across the street.

"Kate, that's dangerous, as well as illegal."

"But I needed to talk with you," Kate said. She stopped short in front of Po and repeated the conversation she'd had with Danny Halloran.

"I didn't remember Esther having a child," Po said, "But no one really knew her, so I guess it shouldn't surprise me. I do remember Ella Halloran having her clothes made by someone. The poor dear just couldn't fit into ordinary sizes—not even the pluses." Po thought about Esther Woods, trying to remember if she ever spoke with the woman. Even all these years later, she remembered her at that quilt display, standing shyly beside her masterpiece. But she honestly couldn't remember ever talking with her, except for that night. "Maybe Selma knows something about Esther's daughter. I'm headed in there anyway."

They reached the door to Selma's shop, and Kate followed Po inside. Her hair had dried completely and now poofed out from her head in a thick tangle of waves. She pulled a bright green scrunchie out of her jeans pocket, grabbed a fistful of hair, and pulled it tight, away from her face.

Selma opened early on Mondays for decorators, letting them wander freely with their clients before Selma got busy with regular customers. Several people were already there, walking the aisles of colorful silks and cotton blends and a host of upholstery fabrics that Selma had added in recent months.

In the imported fabric section, Po and Kate spotted Janna Hathaway. She was following a tall, thin woman carrying a notebook.

"Janna must be planning colors for her new house," Po said.

"Or perhaps watching her decorator plan colors for her new house. She doesn't look like she's enjoying it much." Kate watched as Janna's decorator checked tags, compared one bolt to another, and held colors up to the light. Absent was any consulting with Janna, who followed several feet behind her.

"What are you two doing here at this hour?" Selma asked, coming up behind them.

"I need some thread for the Picasso quilt," Po said. "I didn't think you'd mind if I snuck in with the decorators."

"And I'm here to probe the recesses of your memory," Kate said.

"Probe away, Kate, but know that I lose a memory cell every two minutes."

Kate laughed, then repeated once again the conversation with Danny Halloran.

"A daughter," Selma repeated out loud, thinking back to her brief encounters with Esther Woods. "Of course that's possible, but—" She straightened a bolt of fabric, then nodded as her memory cleared. "Yes, Kate. I think I remember now. She came in once to buy some things for Esther. Po, it was when your Sophie was working in here part-time after school. She knew her, or I guess didn't really know her. But knew she was in school with her. She was an odd duck, if I remember correctly."

"Do you remember her name?" Kate asked.

"Now you are pushing the memory limits, Kate," Selma said. "But she was probably about the same age as all you kids. And I don't think she stayed at Crestwood High long, though. Don't know if she went off to a private school or what, though it's hard to think Esther could have afforded that. I think there was some kind of trouble, but I can't remember exactly what."

Kate nodded. That fit with Danny's story. She looked over at Po. "Maybe wherever she went, she met Laurel St. Pierre. Maybe that's how she got the quilt?"

A customer called for attention at the cash register, and Kate took a step backwards to let Selma through, bumping into someone standing directly behind her.

"Oh, I'm sor—," Kate began, then looked up into Janna's embarrassed face. "Oh, Janna! I didn't see you standing there. I hope I didn't kill your foot. I think it's these shoes." She started down at her thick-soled sandals, scolding them with her eyes.

Janna shook her head. "My fault, Kate. I didn't realize you were standing there when I squeezed in to look at this bolt of fabric."

"You're with your decorator?"

"Yes, we're looking for fabrics for our couch and curtains today. I guess I'd better find her," Janna said nervously. Her eyes darted over the rows of fabrics until she spotted the tall women Kate had seen earlier. With a quick nod to Kate, she turned and hurried off.

Kate glanced at the fabric Janna had been fingering. It was a bolt of coarse, black muslin. *Hmm,* Kate thought. *Can't wait to see what their bedroom looks like!*

Po said goodbye to Kate and walked the short distance home. She left the shop with far more on her mind than thread for Picasso's quilt. She couldn't shake the conversation with Kate and Selma about Esther having a daughter close in age to Sophie and Kate. She felt like Selma, losing those tiny pieces of memory, and thought if only she concentrated hard, she'd put the pieces together that would make Laurel St. Pierre's death make sense.

Po didn't want to support Kate's inquiry openly because she knew that brazen as she was, Kate could plunge into dangerous waters without a backward glance. But Po felt Kate was on to something. And finding out how Laurel St. Pierre came into possession of Esther's quilt was a missing link that might help them clear Picasso's name.

But it wasn't until the middle of the night, when she stood at her window thinking about Kate and Picasso and quilts, that she realized just what that link might be.

CHAPTER 18

"Kate, are you teaching today?" Po asked, as soon as it was decent to call Kate. She caught her goddaughter just as she was leaving for Crestwood High and her digital photography class. They call it an *enrichment* class, Kate said. Kids who are interested sign up and come in before school starts.

"I have about twenty kids registered," Kate told Po. "I'm taking an advanced digital class at the college in the afternoon, which works perfectly. I stay one step ahead of the kids."

Po listened politely to Kate's chatter, then asked, "Can I meet you at school when the class is over?"

"Of course. But what's up? I doubt if you've set foot in old CHS since mom and dad dragged you to my graduation." Kate held the cell phone to her ear as she slid into her Jeep and lifted her backpack onto the passenger seat.

"Dragged *you* to your graduation, you mean," Po said. "You were aiming to skip the whole ceremony, if I remember correctly."

"Okay, okay," Kate laughed at the memory. "But seriously, why the visit?"

"I want to talk to you a little more about Esther's daughter," was Po's cryptic answer.

Po arrived at the door of the photography classroom just as class was being dismissed. A noisy gaggle of students poured into the hallway, laughing and whispering teenage secrets. The smells and sounds were just the same as when her own three walked these halls, Po thought. She remembered all those nights in the football stadium praying that David wouldn't lose an arm as he propelled the Crestwood Hatchets to victory. And the honor assemblies for all three of the kids, and the art displays in which her son, Sam Jr., had displayed his fine sculptures. She smiled into the memories and tried to ignore the sweet-sad tug to her heart.

Inside the classroom, Kate sat on the edge of a

desk chatting with a student. She looked up as Po walked in. "Hi, Po. Do you know Amber King? She's one of my favorite students."

"Of course I do," Po said, smiling at the self-composed teenager. "Sophie used to baby-sit for you."

"Hi, Mrs. Paltrow. Sure, I remember. Sophie's the best. She was my role model." Amber shot Kate a quick glance. "And of course you, too, Ms. Simpson."

Kate laughed. "Always the diplomat, Amber."

"And what are you up to, Amber?" Po asked.

"Well, graduation—then off to Northwestern. Journalism, I guess. And for the here and now, I'm working like crazy on the CHS yearbook."

"Amber is editor," Kate added.

"Then this is definitely a serendipitous moment," Po said. "I came up here to see if Kate and I could snoop in your yearbook archives to find an old student."

"As any self-respecting journalist will tell you, snooping is both our pleasure and our forte," Amber said. While Amber's stature and conversation were definitely beyond her years, her giggle was pure teenager and brought smiles from both Po and Kate.

"Then we've come to the right person," Po said.

"Most definitely," Amber said. "And I happen to have first period free to work on 'The Book,' as we call it, so follow me ladies, and we shall snoop away."

Po and Kate followed her down the wide hallway, empty of students now and filled with a tomb-like silence as students settled down to first-period classes.

"Takes you back, doesn't it?" Kate whispered to Po in the hushed voice the halls seemed to demand.

Po nodded. "How many times did your mom and I come up here to find out what you or my kids were up to?"

"Lots, I would guess," Kate said. "Gads, that was a lifetime ago."

Amber opened the door that led into a room filled with long tables cluttered with photos and pieces of paper. Along the wall, another long table held several computers. "Welcome to Yearbook 101," she said. "This is where I've been living for the past year. And there's our elegant archives room." She pointed to a door leading into a tiny room that was once a walk-in closet. "Just turn on the light and snoop away."

Po followed Kate into the small room. They scanned the walls, looking at the bookshelves crammed with yearbooks, memory collections, and other historical documents. "Okay, Kate," Po said, rubbing her palms down the sides of her jeans, "let's have a go at it. What year did Nancy, Sophie, and Maggie graduate?"

Together they pulled down four or five books covering the years before and after the graduation. "They were all seniors when I was a freshman," Kate said, as she blew dust off the cover of one of the books. "I remember looking up to those kids. P.J. would have been a junior. Funny that none of us can remember Esther's daughter."

Po pulled another book off the shelf. She flipped through it and found her daughter's picture. "High school was a good time for Sophie—but not my boys. Sam Jr. and David couldn't wait to move on. Kind of like you, Kate." She smiled at Sophie's senior picture.

Kate nodded. "High school wasn't my favorite world. But there were good moments."

Po and Kate collected a half-dozen books and took them out to the larger room, spreading them out on the table.

"Okay, I'll start with the senior year. Why don't you take the year before?"

Together Kate and Po poured through the books, looking for Esther Woods' daughter. In Nancy and Sophie's class there were two Woodses—a football player named Jerrod, and a petite girl named Shelly who wore broad-rimmed glasses. "I know Shelly Woods—she lived behind us," Kate said, when Po pointed to the picture. "Her older sister babysat for me."

"We're assuming the Woods girl was in the

same class as the girls," Po said. "But that might not have been the case. Selma just said she was in school *about* the same time."

"I was a freshman when Sophie was a senior—but I don't remember *any* upper classman except for Sophie and Maggie's group. I was treading fiercely just to learn my way around the school."

Kate pored through the senior photos from a year later but the name Woods didn't show up in that class, nor the two years after that.

"Let's go back to Sophie's year and check underclassmen. If she left Crestwood, like Danny said, she might not have had a senior picture."

Kate began looking at the smaller pictures of the junior class, then moved to sophomores. Although Crestwood had less than 25,000 residents, it only had one high school. And busses still brought many students in from the surrounding areas, making it one of the larger schools around.

"The only class left is mine. I don't remember a Woods, but who knows? I don't remember much from that year." Po and Kate leaned over the table and together looked at the small photos as Kate turned the pages.

"There!" Kate pointed to a small picture at the edge of a row. *Ann Woods,* the type beside it read. "What do you think, Po? Could that be Esther's daughter?"

Po picked the book and looked closely at the

picture. "Ann Woods. Does she look familiar to you, Kate?"

Kate squinted at the picture and tried to pull the plain features of the girl in the photo from her memory. She had medium brown hair, a slightly pocked complexion. She looked like a million other kids, Kate thought. Plain and forgettable. The one distinguishing factor was the blouse she wore. It was white, with an old-fashioned collar. And on each wide lapel was an embroidered design.

Po took the book from Kate and looked closely at the picture. "Look at that, Kate." The tip of her nail touched the collar of the blouse. "Does that look like a bird to you? I think we may, indeed, have found Esther's daughter."

As tiny as it was, they could distinguish the shape of a bird appliquéd on the blouse collar. "It's probably beautiful," Kate said. "But imagine how Ann Woods must have hated it then. It couldn't be further from the black sweaters, jeans, and t-shirts that made up my high school wardrobe."

"Well, you weren't exactly run-of-the-mill, Kate." Po laughed, remembering Kate's constant bouts with conformity and how Po and Kate's mother used to cringe when Kate brought home her finds from the used-clothing stores.

"But I would never have worn a hand-made blouse. Nobody would have. It was inviting ridicule, Po."

"You're right. I wonder if Esther made her dress that way. Such a shame. It must have made her life difficult."

Amber moved away from the computer where she was finishing up the editor's page and looked at the picture. "That's hard to see, isn't it? Here—" She checked the date on the yearbook, then opened a metal cabinet and dug through it until she found the right CD. She walked back to her computer, slipped the CD into a slot and clicked on the icon that popped up on the screen. Kate and Po stood behind her, watching the screen while Amber found the same page of photos, focused in on one with her cursor, and enlarged it.

"There, better?" she asked. "We had film of old class books and have started putting them all on CDs to preserve them a little better. Of course, everything is digital now, so we'll have it all neatly stored from the beg—"

"Oh my lord," Kate said, interrupting. Her eyes were glued to the photo on the screen. "Now I remember her." She leaned over Amber's shoulder and pointed at the picture that loomed large in front of them. "Kids called her Carrie— after that Stephen King movie. She never smiled, like in the picture, maybe because her teeth were terribly crooked. I always wanted to nab her parents and give them the name of the orthodontist mom and dad made me go to. It made me mad that her folks wouldn't do some simple things that would make her look a little better so the kids wouldn't make fun of her."

Po looked closer, then squinted, as if shifting the photo into a different kind of focus. She stepped back. "Amber," she said softly, "can you make Ann Woods a redhead?"

"Sure," Amber said. "Photoshop is my second name."

In minutes the plain brown-haired girl on the screen was turned into a redhead.

"Now some color to her cheeks," Po said. "And even out her complexion. Maybe smooth the hair a little and straighten out the nose."

Kate stared. She saw it now, too, and knew exactly where Po was headed. And somehow it wasn't a surprise.

Amber moved a small paintbrush across the pocked face, and in seconds, the Carrie-like young woman had disappeared.

Ann Woods wasn't Ann Woods any longer. Ann Woods was Laurel St. Pierre.

CHAPTER 19

Kate and Po stared at the picture.

Po shook her head. "I think I've known we were headed this way for awhile. But I couldn't connect the dots quite right."

"Remember when I said Laurel stared at me sometimes? Now I understand. She probably thought I was 'one of them'—all those kids who teased her mercilessly."

"The poor dear girl. What a life she must have had back then."

"Didn't Selma say her mom sent her away to get away from the father?" Kate couldn't take her eyes off the class picture. Laurel's beauty was hidden, but it was there, behind the sad eyes and the angry set to the narrow jaw. "Imagine, Po, having to send your own daughter away at that age. I think of you and mom, of Sophie and me. It's unimaginable. It must have been so hard for Esther. But why did she let Picasso bring her back here, to all those memories of that sad life. Do you suppose Picasso knows about all this?"

"Or the police? I think we'd better find out."

Within the hour, Kate and Po had found P.J. He was sitting on the small deck of the old carriage house he rented just south of Po's home. He wore sweats and a t-shirt, still damp from his morning run, and was reading the morning paper.

Without much discussion and ignoring P.J.'s frown at their investigative fervor, Kate dropped the yearbook in his lap, and then handed him a copy of the photo Amber had doctored with Photoshop, transforming the plain Ann Woods into the glamorous woman who had married Picasso St. Pierre. She followed it with a brief explanation. Danny Halloran said Esther sent

152

her daughter away—there was trouble, he said.

"So now the police'll have a new direction in which to go," Kate said as P.J. stared at the pictures in his lap. "Maybe there's a police report or something about the dad causing trouble, the mom sending her away." Unsaid, but as clear as the spring sky, were the words: *And leave our friend Picasso alone.*

"I remember Ann Woods now," P.J. said, pointing at the yearbook photo. "I felt sorry for her. Guys used her mercilessly. I remember her sitting alone in the football stands when we'd be playing. She was always there, always staring at the team. I think she had a crush on someone, but no one would own up to it. They'd just point and laugh. Once I heard a bunch of seniors challenge one of the guys to 'have her' as they so crudely put it. Nasty stuff. I can't believe she's the glamorous Laurel St. Pierre."

"Believe it," Kate said, patting him on the shoulder. She pecked him on the cheek, then followed Po as she started back down the short flight of deck stairs.

"Where are you two headed now?" P.J. called over the railing. The newspaper flapped in his hand and his voice held a note of anxiety, as if he didn't really want to hear their answer.

"To see Picasso before he hears this new development on the news," Po said. "That seems to happen these days with frightening speed."

153

Picasso was already at the restaurant, his apron tied tightly around the bulge of his stomach. A cast iron frying pan simmered on the stove, filling the room with the smell of onions and garlic and fresh, pungent basil.

"Oh, Picasso, I'm dying," Kate said, grabbing a hot pad and lifting the lid.

"You must come tonight and dine. I have sea scallops today—pan roasted—and as round and plump as a baby's cheek." He walked up beside Kate and stirred the onions with a long wooden spoon while Kate held the lid. "To the sauce I will add bacon and cream, a splash of fine vermouth." His eyes closed as he envisioned the creamy and robust delicacy that would grace his dinner tables that night.

Po noticed that the terrible anxiety of a few days ago was beginning to disappear, and in its place, a saddened, older Picasso took hold, but the chef's passion for fine food and the art of cooking was still there, emerging from the folds of his grief. It's that amazing passion that will pull him through all this ugliness, she thought.

"So why are my two favorite ladies visiting me at this hour?" He put the lid back on the pan and turned the flame down beneath it.

Po ushered him to a small table beneath the window, cluttered with notepaper, pencils and recipe cards. "Let's sit, Picasso," she said, and then began in gentle phrases to tell him about the unexpected lineage of Laurel Woods St. Pierre.

Picasso sat still, listening carefully as Po talked. His eyes never left her face and his hands were still on the tabletop. When Po finished he lifted his chin and looked for a long moment out the window. Finally he drew his gaze back and focused again on Kate and Po. "That explains many things," he said slowly, his eyes shifting from Po to Kate and then back again. "It was Laurel, you know, who wanted to come here to Crestwood. She found the information on this little empty place. 'Kansas?' I said to her. 'Whoever heard of a French bistro in Kansas?'" He forced a smile. "But I loved her, and if she wanted to go to the wheat fields, then I would go. She was so secretive here—she said she knew no one—but she was always looking at people, always asking questions. And sometimes an anger gripped her so mightily, and . . ." He stared at the table, his pudgy fingers drawing invisible circles on the wood.

"And what, Picasso," Po prompted.

"That anger, it would come back and attack me. I didn't mind. Sometimes it left her feeling better, I think, when she could scold me and accuse me of things, and even, once, she called the police to say I was hurting her." His voice drifted off and he seemed to be reliving moments with his disturbed wife.

Po and Kate sat quietly, remembering the police report.

"I would never have lifted a finger—or even a voice—to cause her a second of pain, you know. But she had these headaches, and I was the one who was there."

"Did she ever mention her parents, Picasso?"

He shook his head. "Only slightly, only enough that told me her father was a bad man whom she hated. Her mother was a weak woman, but Laurel loved her fiercely. She talked sometimes about her mother's death—and it always caused headaches and confusion."

"Confusion?" Kate asked.

"Sometimes she would talk about getting even. She never would talk about why or who—but here in Crestwood she was sometimes rude and awful to good people—like Max Elliott, my friend."

"Why, Picasso," Po asked.

"Oh, Po, if only I knew why? She hated Max. I don't know why. And then she had her . . . her dalliances. The wine salesman. And another in New York before him. But she didn't love them, I knew. She loved only me."

Po reached out and covered his hand with her own. His fingers quieted and his smile returned to his face. "She was complicated, my Laurel."

On Picasso's other side, Kate sat still. She knew they had only cracked the surface of who Laurel

156

St. Pierre was, but the pain she caused this sweet man was creating havoc with her emotions.

"I think Laurel came here for a reason, Picasso," Po said. "And I think when we find that out, we may be closer to who murdered her, and we'll be able to banish this awful cloud and make you whole again."

Picasso smiled sadly. He nodded and said softly, "With friends like you, I will be fine." Then he pushed back his chair and walked across the kitchen to attend his sauce, wondering if a fine baby beet salad with creamy goat chevre, a sprinkling of micro greens, perhaps, would be the perfect accompaniment for his succulent, caramelized scallops. *Yes,* he thought. *It would be an excellent choice.*

CHAPTER 20

Phoebe decided a Thursday-night quilt gathering was in order, and e-mailed everyone to meet in Selma's backroom at 7:30. They needed to check up on the progress of Picasso's quilt—and on their lives, she wrote.

News of Laurel St. Pierre's real identity had stunned the town, and stories of Ann Woods were rampant.

"Now it's clear why Laurel stared at Kate in the restaurant," Maggie said, looping one leg over a chair. "She was in your class, Kate. She was probably waiting for you to recognize her. Don't you remember ever meeting her?"

"Mags, there were over 300 kids in my class," Kate reminded her.

"That's right. And freshmen are such scared creatures," Maggie said.

"I don't remember ever seeing Ann around town," Eleanor said. "But I did talk to Esther now and then when I took sewing to her."

"The thing I can't get off my mind is that her mother sent her away," Phoebe said. "It sounds like all Esther Woods had of value was her daughter, and then for some reason the daughter disappears when she's, like what, 15? Why would a mother do that?" Phoebe thought about her own precious twins, and deep, disapproving furrows wrinkled her brow. She brought her coffee cup over to the table and sat down.

"She sent her away to protect her from the father," Eleanor reminded her. "That's a heroic thing, though an awful situation. And how miserable that there wasn't anything in place back then to protect Esther and get her help from that abusive man."

"Bill McKay is trying to get some tax money to build a place for women just like Esther," Phoebe said. "So things are changing, finally."

"Good for Billy," Eleanor said. "He seems very tuned in to what this town needs." Eleanor sat at the end of the table, her cane at her side and a bright silk jacket keeping away the cool spring air.

"Yes, but unfortunately it's too late to help Esther Woods," Po said. She had racked her brain for two days, trying to dredge up any memories she might have had of the Woods family, but came up empty, except for one thing—the amazing quilt—the soaring bird and vital life that poured from the golden stitches that held it together. Esther Woods could certainly have used a friend. And usually Po and Liz Simpson happened upon people like Esther and would help out in some small way. But Esther Woods had slipped through the cracks of their lives.

Po pulled out the fabric blocks she was working on. They were already shaping up into a smooth black pot—formed from fabric with subtly patterned swirls of black and gray and navy.

"Po, your pot is looking good," Leah said, looking over her shoulder. She pushed aside some scissors and pieces of fabric and placed her nearly completed fish on the table. "Let's see how they look together."

"Leah, that's magnificent!" Maggie said, standing to get a better look at the large vibrant fish that Leah had created. It was now far more than the silhouette they had seen last Saturday. Today the fish was covered with scales made out of small pockets of fabric, filled with light batting. They overlapped artfully on the body of the fish, small patterned flaps of warm colors—fire brick, sliding into maroon, dark reds and sandy, chocolaty browns. Toward the head the fins moved into rosier tones—coral and salmon and a rust-colored pattern that would complement the rough-textured walls in Picasso's restaurant. "Susan's is similar," Leah said, "but in a different color palette."

Susan pulled her fabric out of a large sack and displayed her small cutout fins in shades of orchid and plum, and thistle, and cobalt blue. The tip of the tail, already completed with the neat rows of small fabric pockets, was fashioned of slippery fabric in shades of dark magenta and purple. "We'll appliqué them onto the pieced background, then quilt around them so they'll stand out."

"Flying fish," Po said.

"Just what Picasso wanted," Kate added.

"We're wonderful!" Phoebe said.

"And not only that, we've enough done now that people will get a really good look at the finished product when I display it tomorrow night. Maggie and Phoebe have some of the border done—and Eleanor, your background blocks look great. I'm going to lay it all out on that display bed I have out front."

"Great idea, Selma," Susan said as she lifted the pieces of her quilt from the table.

"This weekend is alumni weekend at

Canterbury," Leah added, "so you'll have lots of people in, Selma. The timing is perfect."

"I should have the pot completely finished, I think," Po said. "At least I hope to." She thought of the chaos of the last two weeks, and how regular routines and plans had been tossed to the wind. Laurel's death had been like a Kansas tornado, ripping through the small town. Picasso's quilt provided therapy for all of them, and she only hoped by the time it was finished, Laurel's murderer would be found, and lives could return to normal.

Even Hoover sensed the restlessness in his owner, and he crawled up beside Po on the couch later that evening, spreading his golden body comfortably over the forest green upholstery and flopping his head on her lap, directly on top of the morning paper. Max Elliot was expected soon—Po's lawyer and friend—who needed some routine papers signed and had offered to stop by with them on his way home. So reading seemed a better option than delving into the dozens of other things on her plate—like finishing the pot or working on an article that was almost finished. Dear Max, whose name was being tossed around with increased frequency in the muddy waters of this mystery.

"Hoover," Po scolded. "You know better." But her mood and the comfort of the golden retriever's presence overshadowed the golden clumps of fur he'd leave on her couch, and she patted his head. Po was distracted anyway, her thoughts scattered, and the dog's presence had a grounding effect.

The fact that a killer was loose, maybe in their own town, was never far from Po's mind these days, though neither she nor the other Queen Bees alluded to it much. She worried about Kate—and that impulsive streak that sometimes took her into dangerous spots. Po had celebrated P.J's reentry into Kate's life, not only because she liked him so much, but because he brought a more cautious element into her goddaughter's life, a kind of protectiveness that Kate would absolutely deny, but that Po knew was real.

Po glanced down at the part not covered by Hoover's head, and a headline loomed large: "Local woman lived in fear and shame."

The reporters for the *Crestwood Daily* were more interested in pulling up tales of Al Woods' many arrests and drunken brawls and the horrors for Ann and Esther Woods, forced to live in such an environment, than who had killed the young woman and her lover. They'd even gone so far as to badger Bill McKay for quotes, pushing him to speed up the development of the home for abused women, as if there were hundreds of other women in Crestwood needing a haven—and, Po thought, as if that would bring Esther Woods or her daughter back.

But Bill was taking it graciously, Po had to admit, and was promoting the country club fundraiser for the cause. He and Janna would be honorary co-chairs, the paper read. The event was being put together hastily, probably an effort on someone's part to focus attention on a good thing, rather than the sordid goings-on regarding the murders.

A light knock and the opening of the front door announced Max Elliott's arrival, and Po pushed Hoover to the floor and stood up. Since Sam's death, she had been more than comfortable to have Max know all the intricacies of her financial and legal affairs. She felt safe, knowing his fine mind was watching over things for her. But when he'd called to bring the papers by today, she realized with a start, that for all her denial of Max Elliott having anything to do with the Laurel St. Pierre affair, she felt a slight twinge, a wondering, of how he could possibly fit into Laurel's tangled life.

"Po, you really need to start locking your doors," Max said, walking on into the family room. He pecked Po on the cheek, then bent to greet Hoover.

"Maybe you're right. I'm certainly not afraid, but the atmosphere around town is a little anxious, I must admit." She pushed up the sleeves of her long-sleeved yellow sweater that topped a pair of comfortable jeans. "And perhaps you're just the tonic I need tonight, Max, with all these awful goings on."

"Tonic, eh? I've been called a lot of things, but that's a new one." While Po fixed each of them a small glass of Scotch, Max took the papers out of his briefcase and set them on the coffee table. "You mean about Picasso's wife and that wine fellow, I presume. Awful, awful stuff."

"Yes, it is. And it's even more awful that anyone could consider Picasso mixed up in it."

"I agree. I respect Picasso. He's a good man, a friend. Bad coincidences, is what it is. Damn bad."

Po sat down, slipped her glasses on, and picked up a couple of the papers, scanning the numbers and reading the columns as Sam had taught her to do. "There are others who had motives," Po said, her thoughts still with Picasso.

"I don't doubt it."

"Max, Laurel let it be known to several people that she didn't exactly like you."

Max looked up from the papers. For a minute he didn't say anything, and when he finally spoke, his voice was stern and hard. "Laurel was a bad person, Po."

Po looked at the quiet, gentle man who was trusted with more family secrets than anyone in the town. As long as she'd known him, she'd never heard Max Elliott say a mean word about anyone.

"I know she disliked me. I'm not really sure why," he continued. "I guess it could have been for a couple of reasons. She was rude and impolite, but I tried to ignore it for Picasso's sake."

"Why do you think she was bad for Picasso?"

"Laurel wanted to leave Crestwood," Max said. "Picasso and I had a meeting one day, shortly before she died. He was very upset. Laurel had told him that in a few weeks, she'd be ready to move on. Just as he was experiencing real success here with his restaurant. Just as his reputation was being cemented. But that lady didn't give a tinker's dam. Just wanted to move on, she told him."

"To where? Was Picasso going with her?" Po scribbled her name on several forms and pushed them across the table to Max.

Max swallowed a swig of Scotch and shook his head. "I don't know where she wanted to go, and I don't think Picasso was invited. But that didn't matter—he would have followed that woman to the ends of the earth. And she'd have destroyed him piece by piece along the way. That much I know for sure."

Po sat still for a minute, unnerved by the force of Max's anger. Then she rose and refilled each of their drinks. "We're done with the paperwork, Max," she said, changing the subject. "A short while on my back porch will be good tonic for both of us."

But as they sat in companionable silence, Max's harsh words about Laurel St. Pierre settled uncomfortably inside her head. And running through her thoughts was something Max had told her several months before. His love for French food had pushed him to do something he'd never done before, he'd told her. He'd gone and invested a goodly amount of his retirement in Picasso's French Quarter restaurant.

And one thing Po was quite sure of—a French restaurant without its French cook was not a recipe for success—or for a successful retirement.

CHAPTER 21

The French Quarter wasn't open for lunch on Fridays, so Kate and Po settled for a piece of Marla's spinach quiche. Kate had called Po early that morning and announced that if she was ever going to get a good night's sleep again, they had to meet and figure this Picasso mess out. There were far too many things happening, and all the threads were left dangling, like a very poorly constructed quilt.

Marla was in the kitchen when they arrived, so they were able to find an empty table near the back and place their order without having to hear a rambling dissertation on the day's gossip.

"I see what Leah meant about this weekend being crowded," Kate said, looking around at the small, packed bakery. Many middle-aged couples, some joined by college students, filled the tables and booths, and Kate could see a line forming outside. "We got here just in time."

"Alumni weekend is always packed. Sam and I used to love it. We'd see old friends, and meet parents of students we had gotten to know. Kids were excited about summer being just around the bend, and it was always a happy, upbeat few days."

"Well, at least Selma should have a good crowd tonight. And Picasso, too. Good."

A waitress appeared with two platters of quiche, Marla's homemade sourdough rolls, warm with a crisp crust and plenty of creamy butter to slather on them. Without asking the two frequent customers, the young waitress poured them each a tall glass of ice tea with a slice of lemon and sprig of mint.

"I talked to P.J. last night," Kate began. "He said the police are checking into everything, trying to tie Ann Woods to something here. But he said from what's been gathered so far, Ann never returned to this town until she reappeared as Laurel St. Pierre. Her parents' accident was just a couple of months after she left."

"So there was no need to come back," Po said. "Poor girl—what an awful thing."

"Don't get emotional, Po. We've a murder to figure out," Kate scolded, and pulled out a notepad from her purse. "And besides, from all accounts, Laurel St. Pierre was not a nice girl."

Po nibbled on a roll, listening to Kate and thinking about a fifteen-year-old losing both parents, living with relatives wherever it was she went off to, and the agony of it all. Laurel may not have been nice, but she had also missed growing up in a nurturing family like her own kids, and Kate, too, had.

Kate tapped her pencil on the pad. "Okay, here're some of the things we know—and you jump in, too, Po."

"Writing things down is a good idea, Kate. Sometimes it's easier to see what's missing from the puzzle when you lay the pieces out in front of you."

"Okay," Kate said, "here's what we have: Two people dead."

Po picked up the conversation while Kate wrote. "Jason Sands, Laurel's lover. According to your recollection, Kate, and the conversation I overheard with him and Picasso, Jason had had an affair with Laurel, but he was ready to end it right before she died."

"Why did he want to end it?"

"Maybe Jason was simply tired of her. I think Laurel was just one of many in Jason's long history of affairs. He was probably ready to move on."

"But Laurel wasn't."

"Or would have liked to have moved on with him," Po said.

"When it was just Laurel dead, Jason seemed a likely suspect," Kate said.

"I agree. But with him dead, too, the most likely suspect on first glance is Picasso."

"But he's innocent," Kate said, and wrote INNOCENT on the piece of paper after Picasso's name. "So who had a motive?"

"There's Andy Haynes—" Po began.

"No, not Andy!" Kate said.

"Kate," Po said calmly, "We need to put everyone down, even people we know in our hearts are not guilty. So whether you want to or not, Andy needs to be on the list. He was crazy about Laurel, he wanted to protect her. He probably hated Jason Sands and may have even seen first-hand their flirtations with one another and Jason Sands using her. And Laurel confided in Andy, flirted with him, and egged him on in his young ardor for her. That can make a young man crazy."

Kate nodded and reluctantly wrote Andy's name down.

"Max Elliott had invested in Picasso's restaurant. He knew Laurel wanted to leave Crestwood, and if Picasso had gone with her, it would probably have ruined his retirement savings. So he had motive."

"Max Elliot?"

"I like Max very much, but Laurel, for some reason, hated him. We can't ignore that, no matter how little we thought of her. And then on top of that, there was the restaurant connection," Po warned.

Kate bowed her head and dutifully wrote Max's name below Andy's.

Po took a bite of her quiche, then continued. "We should probably add the woman Jason Sands got pregnant—she had reason to kill both of them. In fact, P.J. told me that Sands had her down as his beneficiary, though he didn't have much other than the house."

Kate added her name to the list.

A shadow fell across the table and Kate and Po looked up into Marla's smiling face. "Greetings, ladies," she said. "Quiche good?" She lifted her heavy brows above large brown eyes, waiting for an answer.

"Of course, Marla. It's always amazing," Po said. "Looks like you've quite a crowd today that agrees with me."

"Those alumni folks have been packing in here since seven o'clock this morning, along with my regulars. It's great. I had a reporter in here, too, asking lots of questions about Picasso and that wife of his."

Po frowned. "What kind of questions?"

"Wanted to know if I knew Picasso well. If they argued much. And she asked about other people, too. Wanted to know who didn't like Laurel—or whatever her name was. I laughed at that one. 'Who did?' I asked her back."

"I didn't know you didn't like Laurel, Marla."

"She was a pain in the behind, if you know what I mean. Pretty bossy, that one. Always watching people, snooping around. Nope, I didn't like her one bit. None of the shop owners did. Well, except Jesse, maybe."

"Jesse?" Kate looked at her strangely. They all knew that Jesse and his business partner Ambrose Sweet, co-owners of Brew and Brie, were also partners in real life. So it clearly couldn't be a romantic thing with Jesse and Laurel. Odd, Kate thought. But she had seen them together. At the time she thought it was nice that Laurel was getting to know the other shop owners.

"Laurel was always leaving the restaurant and hanging out with Jess," Marla went on. "Believe me, Ambrose didn't like it one bit. And she didn't like Ambrose, either. Cut him down in front of Jesse more than once."

"Did Picasso know that Laurel and Jesse were friends?" Po asked.

Marla shrugged. "Beats me, but he had to have been blind not to have seen those two with their heads together, sitting out on the bench laughing like they were high school kids. I'd have thought Jesse was smitten with her, if I hadn't known better."

A waitress summoned her with a wave, and Marla waddled off to deal with the most recent kitchen crisis.

"I like Jesse," Po said. "Always have. He's a sensitive young man, and my guess is he was a good ear for Laurel. Nothing more or less."

"I agree. But would Ambrose know that? He's a jealous fella, Po. I've seen the look on his face sometimes. He doesn't like it when Jesse talks to *me*."

"Well, I guess we can add Ambrose to the list. And Marla, too, though I've heard her talking that way about lots of people, and I haven't seen her pushing any of them into the river."

"Portia Paltrow, what a pleasant surprise." The familiar voice came from behind Po's left shoulder, and she turned around, looking up into the face of Meredith Mellon, an elegant woman about Po's age.

Po and Kate both greeted the tall, attractive woman. Meredith Mellon was Phoebe's mother-in-law, but any similarity between the two women ended right there. Meredith was magazine perfect—a blonde-streaked chignon fastened perfectly at her neck, her tan skin flawless. She was active in many community affairs, and was featured so often in the society pages of the local paper that Po often wondered what Meredith and Phoebe would possibly have to talk about at family dinners.

It took a second for Po to notice Janna Hathaway standing in Meredith's shadow.

"Janna, hello. I didn't see you standing there. Do you know Meredith?"

Meredith answered for her. "We're planning the charity event for the new SafeHome," she said proudly. "I'm chairing the event, and Bill and Janna are our honorary chairs. You're both coming, of course," she said, taking in both Kate and Po. "Phoebe will certainly be there."

Meredith Mellon spoke in declaratives. Phoebe would be coming to the country club event. The "or else" was silent, but was there as loud and clear as the spoken words. Po felt a rush of sympathy for her young blonde quilting friend.

"I'm sorry to rush off," Meredith continued. "Janna and I have finished our business, and I've another appointment. But don't forget to save next Saturday evening for the social event of the season." She turned toward Janna and pecked her on the cheek, then wove her way through the crowded restaurant toward the front door.

Janna watched her walk off, then turned back to Kate and Po. "I hope you both will come. It will be a terrific event—Meredith is amazing—and it's for such a good cause."

Po watched the plain young woman and wondered if she enjoyed the role of public wife. There was an oddness about her that made Po think she actually might like it. But whether to please someone else, or herself, was not entirely clear. "It sounds like a lovely party," Po said.

"Was Meredith leaving us a choice?" Kate said.

Janna shrugged. "Meredith Mellon is much like my mother. So no, you probably have no choice." She managed a small smile. "The event will be a good thing for Bill. The more visibility he gets, the better it will be for his political career."

And that was probably the answer to her thoughts, right there, Po decided. Janna was doing this for Bill, and would probably do just about anything for her husband-to-be. Meredith Mellon's event was a stepping stone, nothing more. "Would you like to sit with us, Janna? We're probably good for one more glass of tea," Po said.

Janna shook her head. "Thank you, but I have to meet Bill and Max Elliot to sign some papers on the house, and also to talk about another project we're considering out on the edge of town—a new, exclusive shopping center. My father is thinking of investing in it, too—he's so proud of Bill." Mention of her father and Bill in the same breath brought a radiant smile to Janna's face, and for a second, Po thought she looked beautiful.

Janna turned to leave, then glanced down at the table and noticed the pad of paper beside Kate's plate. *INNOCENT* popped off the white page. Janna looked at it curiously. "What's this?" she asked.

It was a slightly nosy question, Kate thought. But she felt an undefined pity for Janna Hathaway, so she swallowed the quick retort that sprang to her lips and, instead, explained the frustration she and Po felt because of the unsolved murder.

"Bill said the police are making progress," Janna said

"Maybe. But they still have Picasso in the lineup."

"But along with others, right? Bill said he talked to the police chief and they are thinking that the murderer might even be from New York, someone Laurel maybe jilted—just like she was doing to Picasso. Someone who came back to get even and lured her out to the park that night. Then came out of the bushes by the bridge and pushed her off that rocky ledge into the river. It kind of makes sense. And Bill said they might never be able to find that person, since Laurel was so secretive about her life."

"But Picasso will never be clear of the shadow of her death if the crime isn't solved," Po explained. "Nor will the town be able to easily move on. Closure is important, Janna."

Janna rubbed arms. "It's just so . . . so awful to think about. Especially when there are so many *good* things going on." Janna looked at Kate and Po hopefully, as if happy thoughts would erase the horror of murder. "There's the benefit coming up, for one thing," she said. "And building the SafeHome, and planning for, well, for the wedding." She looked down at the floor. "I know that sounds selfish, but I wish all these bad things would go away."

"I understand, Janna," Po said. "You're absolutely right—the benefit is a good, positive thing, and probably more people will go and contribute to the home because of these awful events. But we still need to exonerate Picasso from all blame."

Janna listened, but both Po and Kate sensed her impatience. And it was understandable, Po thought. She didn't know the people involved, and she had a wedding and new house to prepare. She didn't want anything marring those important events in her life.

"Po's right. We need to bring some closure to it for Picasso's sake, if not our own," Kate said, speaking slowly, as if to a child. Janna's distress over the murder's effect on her important life events was childlike, innocent, and irritated Kate no end. "We think that exploring Ann Woods' past a little, finding out who she really was and what happened to her in the years away from Crestwood, will help us."

"Janna," Po added, "you have plenty on your mind right now, with the charity event, your wedding and house. You worry about them, and Kate and I will take care of Picasso."

Janna stood beside the table, awkwardly fingering her Kate Spade bag.

Kate watched her shift from one foot to another, wanting to stay and wanting to go at the same time. Murder had probably never been this close to her carefully protected life. But Crestwood was a small town that took care of its own, and one person's business, for better or worse, was everyone's business.

And for right now, concern for Picasso topped even Janna Hathaway's wedding, her house, or the Crestwood Country Club event.

CHAPTER 22

P.J. and Kate stopped by Po's that night before heading for a movie in Kansas City. The Crestwood Cinema was sometimes a little behind in first run movies, but the nearby Missouri city easily filled in the gaps. Besides, an evening stroll on Kansas City's Country Club Plaza, enjoying the crowds and music groups gathered around the fountains, would take them a world away from the rumors and worries of the Crestwood murders, something they both needed.

Po was out on the porch with Maggie, sharing a pitcher of martinis and enjoying the warm southern breezes that portended a delightful May.

"Hey, you two," Maggie called out in greeting. "Join us."

"Where's Leah?" Kate asked. "I thought she was joining you?"

"She's being a good-hearted person and helping Selma out. Tonight is first Friday, and Selma was expecting quite a crowd." Po handed P.J. and Kate each a glass. Kate looked beautiful tonight, Po thought. A black pair of stretch pants showcased her long legs, and a deep cobalt blue jacket fit snugly over her white t-shirt. Her cheeks were flushed and her eyes bright. Po looked at P.J. His eyes were on Kate, his tall body relaxed and comfortable in jeans and a light tan jacket. *They look happy together,* Po thought with a jolt. *That's what's happening here. Happiness.* It was more welcome to Po than the bright yellow daffodils popping up beneath the giant pines in her yard. A more powerful sign of good days to come than the bright spring moon.

"I stopped by to see Picasso this afternoon," Kate was saying, oblivious to Po's thoughts. "He's hoping for a crowd tonight, too. And he plans on sending everyone over to Selma's to see his quilt-in-progress."

"Great," Po said. "It's good for people to know he has the neighborhood's support."

Kate sat down beside Maggie on the swing. "Picasso also told me he's decided what to do with Laurel's mother's bird quilt—he's offering it to the SafeHome, to auction at that charity event at the country club. It was Bill McKay's idea, but Picasso loved it. Considering all that's happened, he thought it was the right thing to do—and what Laurel would want him to do."

"I'm not so sure about the latter," Po said. "Who knows what Laurel—or Ann—would have wanted? She's such a mystery woman, even in death. But it's certainly a good and generous thing for Picasso to do."

"We've been looking into Ann Woods' past, Po," P.J. said. He leaned against the railing, his back to the yard. "We've confirmed that when she left here those years ago, she went to upstate New York, so she was honest with Picasso about that. She lived in a small town with a maiden aunt, I think, and finished high school. When the aunt passed away—Ann must have been 17 or 18 —she seems to have disappeared, swallowed up in the bowels of New York City. Or at least that's the best we can figure, since that's where she lived when she met Picasso. And Picasso was pretty sure she'd lived there for several years."

Kate repeated Janna Hathaway's conjecture that it could have been someone from that part of Laurel's life who killed her.

"Could be," P.J. said. "And if that's true, we may never find him or her. But I don't think it was."

"Why?" Po asked, though she completely agreed with P.J. and had her own set of reasons. If someone from Laurel's past had wanted to kill her, New York would have been a much better place to do it, not a small town where everyone knew each other and strangers were as noticeable as blue men from Mars. Besides, Laurel's presence and her behavior in Crestwood seemed to be calculated. Po was convinced Laurel had come back for a reason, some sort of revenge. And that reason was right there in their little town. They simply couldn't see it. At least not yet.

P.J. shifted on the porch railing. He seemed reluctant to say why he thought the way he did, but he finally offered, "The dual murders, for one reason. Sands had no ties to the East Coast. He'd never been outside the Midwest and never planned to go. Furthermore, who but a resident would know about those quarries where Sands' body was found? Some people who live here couldn't even find their way down those narrow roads. And Sands had told Picasso he was going to benefit from something Laurel told him. He knew something, and thought that knowledge was worth something."

Po watched P.J.'s angular face as he talked. It was partially lit by the full moon, and the strong lines of his jaw were outlined prominently. P.J. Flanigan is a thoughtful man, she thought. And a kind man. And if Liz Simpson were alive and sitting there with a martini in hand, she'd thoroughly approve of the direction this relationship was heading.

And between P.J. and me, we will keep her safe, Liz, Po promised, suddenly missing her best friend fiercely.

Po wasn't sure that Kate would make it to the Queen Bees Saturday session, knowing she was out late the night before. But sure enough, as Po walked out of Marla's with a grand latte in hand, she spotted Kate rounding the corner in her familiar green Jeep.

Po waved and waited while Kate parked the car and ran across the street.

Kate pecked her on the cheek. "Okay, yes, Po, we had a great time," she said before Po could ask for a report. "He drives me crazy some-times—but other times?" Kate lifted her brows and rolled her eyes mischievously.

Po laughed, then looped her arms through Kate's and together they headed for Selma's. The alumni crowd was even more plentiful today, lining up at Marla's to savor her eggs and coffee. "Too bad Picasso doesn't serve breakfast," Po mused. "He'd make a fortune today."

They looked beyond Picasso's to Selma's store. The door was already open and blinds lifted. As they neared the doorway, Selma stepped out onto the sidewalk and started toward them. Her face was tight, and damp, flyaway gray tendrils curled against her forehead. Bright spots lit her cheeks, the only signs of emotion as she waved them close. "Not a good day, ladies," she said crisply. "I'm glad you're here early."

Po and Kate looked at each other, then followed Selma into the half-lit store. Susan stood behind the counter, a strange, sad look on her face.

Selma gestured toward the west side of the store and Kate and Po looked toward the wall, a freshly-painted white surface ten feet high that was covered with this month's first Friday display—bright, magnificent works of quilting art. Then just as quickly, their eyes lowered to the bed display holding their own creation—Picasso's quilt with the brilliant fish flying into Po's pieced black pot.

Po's hand flew to her mouth. "Oh, Selma—" she moaned.

The fish were still in flight, their bodies placed on the unfinished pieced background. And running along the right side of the quilt, slashing through Leah's fish and dissecting the black pot like a sword, was a thin, wavy river of destruction—a pale yellow-white swoosh that robbed the art of its brilliant crimsons and purples and silvers.

"It's bleach," Selma said quietly.

Susan's eyes filled with tears. "I should have been watching the crowd more closely."

"Nonsense," Selma said. "Who provides surveillance for quilt lovers?

"What kind of monster would do this?" Kate asked.

"What's done is done," Selma said. She looked at Kate. "Come on sweetie, help me with this."

Together Selma and Kate lifted the whole sheet beneath the quilt and carried it into the back room. Selma motioned toward the work table and they laid it there, on the long oak table where various Queen Bees had found friendship for nearly thirty years as they pieced bits of fabric together into quilts.

"I don't want customers to see this," Selma said, her eyes running up and down the bleached-out river. Her hands were knotted into tight fists and she pushed them into her hips, staring at the damage. "I should never have suggested we use it last night. I'm so sorry to all of you. Leah will be appalled."

At the mention of her name, Leah, followed by Maggie and Phoebe, walked in the back door. Wordlessly they surveyed the damage. And then as if on cue, the air was filled with crashing exclamations, outrage, and questions.

"When did you discover this?" Po asked Selma, managing to squeeze her question into a short-lived lull.

"Not until this morning. It was so packed in here last night you could barely move. Picasso's had a line all the way down the block, and the overflow wandered around in here, waiting for their tables. Also, a Canterbury professor's quilts were on display, and students and parents who knew her came in to see it." Selma unpinned Leah's fish from the background fabric and absently, as if telling it that it'd be okay, pressed the fabric to her cheek.

"People were still here at closing," Susan said. "Leah and I turned the spotlights out over the quilts to get people to leave, so it was dark on that side of the room, and we didn't see the streak."

"Well, I have many of my little fins left over—I wasn't sure what colors would fit in best so I made a ton. I can redo my fish without too much difficulty," Leah said.

"And my cauldron just may end up with some vegetables floating around it. There's always a way," Po said.

"But why in heaven's name would anyone have bleach in here? It makes no sense whatsoever!" Phoebe leaned over the damaged quilt, her palms flat on the table.

The room grew quiet as they tried to make sense of the damage. Finally Po asked, "Selma, were you the last to leave?"

"Yes. I sent Susan on her way—she has that drive all the way out to her farm. So I took care of the cash register, straightened a few fabric bolts, and went on home. The cleaning crew arrived when I was leaving."

"Have you talked to them? Could they have spilled something on the quilt?" Po asked.

"I called Jake Hansen this morning as soon as I

discovered it. He's the head man, honest as the day is long. He saw it as soon as they started sweeping, he said. Jake doesn't know diddlysquat about quilts—he thought maybe I had tried some new technique on it, kind of like tie-dye, he said." Selma's laugh was hollow.

"So we know for sure it happened during the show," Po said.

"Is that possible?" Kate asked. "Wouldn't you have smelled the bleach?"

"Not in a room filled with fifty kinds of fancy perfumes and waves of Picasso's garlic shrimp wafting in from down the street," Leah said.

"And it was so crowded that someone with a small spray bottle could easily have gone unnoticed," Susan added. "Besides, the fabric wouldn't have faded immediately, so no one would have noticed it 'til later."

Po ran her fingers along the colorless fabric. She shook her head. "Random acts of violence. It's so difficult to understand."

"Maybe not so random," Selma said.

All the Queen Bees stared at her.

"What do you mean, Selma? If not random, it was aimed at you, or at all of us—it's our quilt. That's ridiculous," Po said.

Eleanor had slipped in the back door and heard the last few minutes of conversation. She walked over and looked at the quilt, shaking her head in dismay.

Selma turned away from the quilt and looked at Po. Her face was composed and thoughtful. "I think it's unlikely someone would walk into a quilt store on a crowded night and risk getting caught in such a foolish act unless there was a deliberate reason for doing it."

"Oh, Selma, I don't think so," Po said. But her words were soft and lacked conviction. Selma's reasoning was far too close to her own to offer vacuous reassurances.

"But why would anyone want to damage our quilt?" Phoebe asked. "If they wanted to do real damage they could have trashed the store or stolen Selma's receipts, or slashed our tires, or—"

"Exactly my point," Selma interrupted. "This was done by someone who knows the effort we put into this quilt, someone who knows how much it means to us. And it was someone who knew that damaging the quilt would get our attention."

Eleanor stood over the quilt, its garish stain running down the side. Her glasses slid down her nose and the sleeve of her elegant silk blouse brushed across the fabric as veined hands touched it reverently. "Damn," was all she said. Her gray head moved slowly moved from side to side.

"And I double that thought, Eleanor." P.J. strode into the room from the archway, his eyes searching for the quilt.

A few scattered hellos greeted him, but the others turned to look at Kate.

She lifted her shoulders in a small shrug. "Okay, I called him," she said. "This freaks me out. I think someone is sending us a message—"

"—to mind your own business," P.J. finished. "May I look?"

Po nodded and stepped aside so P.J. could have a good view of the bleach-damaged fabric. He looked at it from afar, then leaned close, squinting at the circuitous design. "There, see that?" His fingers traced the trail of bleach.

The Queen Bees followed the line of his finger. The path of the bleach was messy, difficult to discern, like a child's first attempt at writing. And some would have disputed it, saying P.J. was reading into it, like a Rorschach Test.

But the Queen Bees could see it, as clear and crisp as a finely pieced and quilted star.

MYOB, it warned.

CHAPTER 23

"We need to talk about this." P.J. walked over and helped himself to a cup of coffee. The women remained at the table, staring at the cryptic message. It jumped out of the quilt now, as clear as any writing they'd ever seen, and each Bee wondered how she could have missed it.

P.J. walked back to the table. "The whole lot of

you has been asking questions all over town. Someone is telling you very clearly to back off."

"But . . ." Phoebe said.

"No 'buts,' Phoebe. This is serious. It makes sense you'd be warned this way. The quilt is for Picasso. And you're all making it. It's a perfect vehicle for a warning."

They stood in silence for a minute, the impact of the quilt damage settling down on them like a thick fog. Kate shivered and pulled her sweater close. Po walked over to the window and stared out into the spring day. It had suddenly turned cold and gray. Fear does that, she thought, robs a life of color.

Back at the table, P.J. spoke into the silence. "How many people know about this quilt?" he asked.

"I told my kids' play group," Phoebe said, "and all the moms that hang out in the park. Not to mention Jimmy's law firm. And his mother knows, which is like telling the whole town. Everyone knows, P.J. You know us."

"I ate at the French Quarter last night and Picasso was telling everyone who came in to come over and look at it," Eleanor said.

"So hundreds, P.J., to answer your question," Kate said.

"Well, I think this act was planned," he said. "Maybe not for days, but longer than the time it takes to get from Picasso's restaurant to here."

He turned to Selma. "Do you remember who was in here last night?"

Selma shook her head. "P.J., there was an army of people in here. Many I knew, sure—neighbors and friends and regular customers. And I'm sure there were plenty of those I didn't even see. Leah and Susan and I mingled in different parts of the store at different times. On an ordinary day I could tell you exactly who came in, but last night was not ordinary. And in addition to faces I recognized, there were all the college visitors, most of them strangers." She shuddered, suddenly. The thought of the murderer being in her store, maybe inches away from her, caused goosebumps to rise on her thick arms. She rubbed them vigorously. "We could look at receipts, P.J., but I don't think that would tell us much. We sold plenty, but the majority of people came to look at the display. And a goodly percentage of them were from out of town."

P.J. nodded. Selma was right. It would be hard after-the-fact to put faces to the event. A needle in a haystack, or, more accurately, in a sewing store.

He thought of Kate, and her obsession with this murder case. It was all she talked about last night on their drive to Kansas City. She was putting herself in danger, along with all the other nice, bright women standing around this room. "The person who killed Ann Woods and Sands would probably kill again if there was a need to do it," he said slowly. "For whatever reason Laurel—Ann—was killed, anyone who gets too close to the truth puts herself or himself in danger. That may have been what happened to Sands. Laurel may have told him something. Maybe he said something to someone. Threatened the murderer. Tried blackmail. And now all of you are putting yourselves out on the line in your efforts to protect Picasso." He looked around the room, then settled his gaze on Kate's lovely face. "Please, back off, all of you. And leave this to the investigators working the case. Please."

When Leah and Po met the next morning for Marla's Sunday special, their appetites weren't up to crispy French toast, stuffed today with fresh mangoes and topped off with a dusting of powdered sugar and river of almond syrup. But they picked away at it, talking quietly about Saturday's quilt episode.

After P.J. called the police in and pictures had been taken of the quilt, the Queen Bees realized it wasn't going to be as easy to repair it as they thought. The police walked off with the section of the quilt that had been damaged, marking it as evidence. Selma immediately went out to the front of the store and found new fabric to replace the missing sections, and by the end of the morning, all the pieces for the body of the appliquéd fish and black pot had been cut and were ready for Leah and Po to work on. It was as if the assault on their quilt propelled the Bees, and what would have taken many hours, was produced out of their anger and frustration in the small space of a morning.

"P.J. seemed worried," Leah said. "That's not like him."

"He'd be concerned anyway, but with Kate involved—and being as impetuous as she can be—he's especially so."

Leah nodded. "Well, he's right. This isn't a game of Clue anymore. It's a murder investigation, after all."

"Yes," was all Po said, and she pushed her plate away, aware of the danger and concerns that shadowed them all.

The bakery seemed especially noisy today, and Po looked around at the crowd. Some of her neighbors sat in the front window, and she spotted Jesse and Ambrose at the table next to them. Their heads were bent in conversation and as Po watched, Ambrose threw down his napkin, pushed out his chair, and abruptly stomped out of the restaurant. Before she could look away, Jesse looked up and saw Po watching him. He smiled slightly, picked up the check, and walked over to their table.

Po looked up into his youthful face. Jesse was in his mid-thirties, but with blonde, floppy hair, slender physique, and a shy, sweet smile that made him look much younger. She and Jesse had had many fascinating conversations over the Brew and Brie's fine cheeses and imported fruits and candies about his travels and love of art. She liked this young man exceedingly. "Jesse, I'm sorry. I didn't mean to be eavesdropping," she said.

Jesse brushed away her apology with a wave of his hand. "It's okay, Po. No matter. Ambrose hasn't been himself lately."

Jesse stood at the side of their table as if he wanted to say something more, but wasn't sure what.

"Would you like to have a cup of coffee with us?" Leah asked.

Jesse seemed relieved at the invitation and pulled out a chair and sat down. "I'm worried about all this Picasso mess," he began, "and I don't have anyone to talk with about it. Ambrose blows up when I mention it. But I need to talk—" He looked at Po, then Leah, his brown eyes sad.

A waitress appeared with a cup of coffee and set it in front of Jesse. "We heard today about your quilt," he said, as the young girl walked away. "Another awful piece to this puzzle."

"You heard about the damage?" Po said. She was surprised and not surprised. The Elderberry neighborhood was tight, and the news of something happening in Selma's shop was bound to leak out.

Jesse nodded. "Marla told us. Ambrose and I were talking with Billy McKay and his fiancé—" he nodded to a table on the other side of the room where Bill and Janna were having breakfast and chatting with the Reverend Gottrey and his wife.

"Marla was upset. And then Billy got upset, too. Real upset. Turned red in the face. People care about all of you Queen Bees."

"It's an uneasy time, Jesse," Po said. "And how are you doing with all of this?"

Jesse looked away, as if collecting his thoughts, not knowing how much he wanted to say. Finally he looked back at Po and Leah and spoke softly. "I loved Laurel. A sweet person emerged from beneath all that anger that defined her. I know how awful she could be. I know she hurt Picasso and hated some people in this town, but it was almost as if there were two people inside her." His eyes filled as he talked about her. "I don't know *how* I loved her, if you know what I mean. That's confusing to me. But I know she was a part of my soul. And the thought that someone could have murdered that special flower blooming inside her is hard to come to grips with."

Po listened and felt an unexpected rush of compassion for him. Whether Laurel's affection for him had been real or fabricated didn't even matter. It had been real to him. "Jesse, I know this must be difficult for you. But I have a question for you. I'm surprised that Laurel hated people in

193

Crestwood. That's such a strong word—hate— and I didn't think she even knew that many people. Who did she know well enough to hate?"

"Laurel didn't need to know people well to hate them, Po. If they crossed her—like Ambrose did—or did anything that offended her, she would cross them off her list. It was just the way she was. But there were people here that she reserved a real strong distaste for. I never understood why. She'd only say that her life would be different if they hadn't messed with it."

"Who was she talking about?" Leah asked.

Jesse shrugged. "Don't really know. She said I didn't need to know. It only mattered that her life had been ruined by people who lived here. It didn't make sense at all because she never told me she had lived here when she was younger. I guess that sheds new light on everything. But I still don't know why she hated people or why she would have come back here." He drained his coffee cup and sat back in the chair. "She'd been really hurt. But she'd never be hurt again, she said. Now she'd be the one doing the hurting. When she talked like that, her eyes turned black and she looked like another person. Almost witch-like," Jesse said, his voice nearly a whisper, as if he could see her standing there in front of him. "It'd be as if she were alone, and she'd mutter to herself. 'No more hatchet jobs,' she'd say."

CHAPTER 24

"What a sad story," Kate said, after Po repeated her conversation with Jesse. It was late, much later than Sunday suppers usually lasted, and most of their friends had left. Po, Kate, and Maggie were alone in the kitchen, finishing up the last dishes. "It almost makes me wish I had known Laurel better. Maybe been able to help her."

"Leah said the same thing. Laurel came close to talking to her a couple times, and now she wished she'd encouraged it. Given her an outlet. Poor Jesse seemed to be one of the few people she confided in." Po wiped her hands on a dishtowel and walked over to the table.

"And Jason Sands," Maggie said.

"But that was different. That wasn't friendship. Picasso said there'd been others like Jason. Some women have a knack for picking abusive, awful men." Po sat down and watched Maggie and Kate finish the last few pots in the sink. Beneath the counter, a full dishwasher whirred comfortingly.

"They were like her father," Kate added. "Some women do that. Abused once, they seem to look for the same kind of men." She wiped a giant platter that had held a whole salmon hours earlier.

Po sipped her cup of tea, then set it down on the

table. "Picasso certainly didn't fit that mold, but I think Laurel picked him for other reasons."

"He gave her security," Kate offered.

"And he gave her what she needed to return to Crestwood on her own terms. He'd have done anything she asked."

"The comment Jesse made, what was it, something about a hatchet. That's a strange thing to say," Kate said.

Po and Maggie agreed. They sat in silence for a few minutes, pondering the day and evening events. Picasso had come to supper—a welcome surprise. He had lost some weight, but in the company of several of the Queen Bees, Gus and Rita Schuette, and P.J., he'd relaxed and even had seconds on the sesame-marinaded salmon that P.J. had prepared on the grill.

At dinner, everyone assiduously avoided the events filling the papers and rumor mill, and conversation had turned to lighter things, including Meredith Mellon's gala event coming up the next Saturday night.

"You will all come, please?" Picasso had asked, and without missing a heartbeat, they'd all agreed wholeheartedly to attend an event that none of the supper guests rated high on their "must do" lists. But for Picasso, they'd go.

Now, in the comfort of Po's kitchen with defenses down, Kate questioned their universal response. "I'd rather scrub my grill," she said, slipping into her jacket and looking around the kitchen for her purse. "I will happily donate to SafeHome. It's a great idea—and Janna and Billy are being generous in their help—but dressing up and being gracious and upbeat right now is maybe more than I can handle."

"Well, it's four hours out of your week, Kate. We can do this for Picasso. Giving that quilt to be auctioned is quite a gesture—it's the one meaningful thing of Laurel's that he owns. He told me that the quilt was her whole life. It won't be easy for him."

Kate nodded. "I know, I know. And Phoebe's thrilled she won't be there by herself."

"Let's just hope by next Saturday we can enjoy ourselves and not be looking over our shoulders to see if there's someone lurking in the shadows or spraying bleach on our clothes," Maggie said, grabbing the keys to her truck off the counter and heading for the back door. "That would be worthy of a celebration, even at Mrs. Mellon's country club."

Kate taught at Crestwood High most of the next week. Sandy Kindred, a teacher who'd taught Kate when she was a student and still taught the same honors English class, always requested her former student to substitute when she couldn't be there. And Kate, in turn, liked the regularity of teaching the same class every day.

"Who knows," she had joked to another teacher, "maybe next year I'll be around permanently."

Kate spent the week caught up in an eerie whirl of reminiscences. Although she'd been around the school for over a year now, subbing and teaching her photography enrichment class, this week was different. And she knew it was because of Ann Woods. Another student who had sat in the same chairs and taken tests on the same desks.

The halls were still familiar, but she felt herself walking them today, not as Kate Simpson, teacher—but as Kate, the freshman, determined not to let any upperclassman get the better of her, determined to be her own person.

She paused in front of the giant bulletin board outside the gym, crammed with graduation notices, "Win with Jane Flynn for STUCO pres" signs, and posters urging the soccer team on to the state finals. "Go Hatchets!" they screamed in giant neon letters—and Kate wondered how many times she had passed Ann Woods in this very spot and never nodded or even said hi.

As the week went on, Kate attacked the shadows of her memory at every change of class, every student announcement, trying to pull back the past. Some events slowly surfaced, but they were always cloudy, thin memories of things like senior boys knocking into Ann, teasing her, flirting with her with macho arrogance, then laughing behind her back. Touching her inappropriately. They'd be sued for sexual harassment today, Kate thought.

On Friday, Kate walked into the teacher's lounge during her free period. She was exhausted for no earthly reason, and was ready for the week to end. Betsy Carroll sat on the old sofa at the far end of the teacher's lounge, reading a book. Betsy had been a counselor and Kate's mentor at Crestwood High when Kate was a student—and she was still doing the same these years later. Kate loved the friendship that had developed in recent months as they got to know one another again, this time as peers.

Betsy looked up as Kate walked over. She smiled and dropped her book on her lap, patting the cushion next to her.

"Flop before you drop, Kate."

Kate grabbed a bottle of water from the small refrigerator and sat down next to Betsy.

"What's up," Betsy asked, sliding her glasses to the top of her head. "You've been distracted all week."

Kate shrugged. She wasn't sure herself what was going on inside her head. It was an uncomfortable nagging, the pea beneath the princess's mattress. "I think it's this whole Ann Woods thing, Betsy. Being back here like this, knowing she and I walked these halls together, maybe sat through old Mrs. Aldrich's algebra class or Goldie Harrison's gym class—and I don't remember it. Don't remember *her*, except for the awful things. Guys teasing her in the cafeteria, girls making fun of her homemade clothes, all that bad stuff. And I keep thinking that if I could remember more, maybe I could put it to rest. Somehow."

"No one knew Ann Woods very well, Kate."

"Do you remember her?"

Betsy nodded. "She was one of my students, just like you were."

"So you counseled her."

"I tried to. Ann didn't talk much, but she started to open up a little at the end." Betsy frowned and looked out the window. Students drifted out onto the sprawling lawn in front of the school, an art class out to sketch the giant elms that shaded the circle drive. It was all so peaceful. Nothing like Ann Woods' time at Crestwood had been. She turned back toward Kate. "You knew that Ann never finished her freshman year."

Kate nodded. "She went to New York State and lived with an aunt."

"I tried to talk her parents out of that. I thought they were doing it just because Ann was having a hard time, being teased and such. I thought if I could just talk to the parents and get her some help, teach her some social skills, help her to dress nicely and fit in a little better, that maybe things would be better for her. I think she wanted to fit in, though she hated the teasing. She was starting to be interested in things around here. She even had a crush on one of the boys on the football team. So I thought maybe we could work it all out."

"But the parents wouldn't listen?"

"They wouldn't even talk to me. Never answered my calls. One day Ann was here, looking sickly and sad. And the next day she was gone."

"And you never saw her again?"

"Once—the day after she dropped out of school. I was coming back from a meeting that night and stopped in at Wally's drugstore down near the river. Ann was on the payphone outside, yelling at someone on the other end of the phone. She was sobbing and yelling, all at the same time. It was frightening."

"Who was she talking to?"

"It was a guy. I heard her tell him she hated him. Her life was ruined, she said. And she told the person that she thought he loved her. And then she dropped the phone and folded up on the floor of the phone booth like a little girl, sobbing as if she were going to die. My heart nearly broke at the sight of her."

"Did she see you?"

Betsy nodded. "She looked up at me, and Kate, I've never seen such sadness. But it was mixed with an anger that I could feel in her thin arms as I helped her to her feet."

"And that was it?"

"Almost. A car pulled up then, nearly running onto the sidewalk. It was that drunken father of hers. He leaned out the car window and yelled for her to get in the car. And then he cursed at her, called her a whore, and mumbled things that didn't make any sense."

"What did he say?"

"He told her that at least this time her 'shacking up,' as he so delicately put it, would be worth his while. He'd make a pretty penny off her getting knocked up, and he'd get rid of her as part of the bargain. His words were slurred, but his message was clear."

CHAPTER 25

"Ann Woods was pregnant?" Kate sat frozen on the couch. For all the bad thoughts she'd had about Laurel St. Pierre, she felt herself drowning in emotion for a fifteen-year-old girl who'd found herself pregnant, alone, and was then disowned and sold down the river by a drunken father.

"Yes, she was. I suspected it about a week before all that happened. She wasn't feeling very good, and she came to me to be excused from gym. The nurse was overloaded so sometimes counselors filled in with those sorts of permissions back then. She didn't tell me she was pregnant, but for the first time since I'd known her, she seemed oddly happy. As if something good was happening in her. Thinking she might have the flu, I suggested she go home. She insisted she was fine, though she was making steady trips to the bathroom in my office. The walls are thin—I knew she was sick."

Kate tried to get her arms around this news about Ann. Pregnant. But what could have happened to the child? She'd be twelve now. Did Picasso know?

"I watched her that week, coming to school each day, with a certain glow about her. But each day she seemed a little less sure of herself, more cautious. And then, like I said before, she came in one morning looking like her life was about to end, and the next day she was gone."

"So she was sent away because she was pregnant, not because her mother was trying to get her away from her father, which was what we all thought."

Betsy nodded. "The poor girl didn't have much of a chance. Her mother loved her, but she was no match for Al Woods."

"Meeting Picasso was the best thing that ever happened to Laurel," Kate said. "That was a chance."

Betsy agreed, but added wisely, "A lot had happened to Ann before she met Picasso. And those things surely shaped the woman she had become. So what she brought to their relationship, why she married him, all of those things were affected by what happened to her right here at Crestwood High."

Kate got up and put her bottle in the recycling bin. "Betsy," she said, slowly turning back to her mentor-turned-friend. "Do you know who the father was?"

Betsy put her book into her purse and rose from the couch. "No, I never knew. There was talk in the teachers' lounge and around school after she left, some rumblings about the crushes she had on older boys. And how they'd lead her on. But Laurel wasn't the kind of girl the kids cared about much—you probably don't even remember when she disappeared from your class."

Kate nodded slowly. That was absolutely right. She didn't notice her absence, except for maybe a fleeting awareness. And she hadn't noticed her presence much, either. *Carrie,* as the older kids called her, *the girl with the weird hair and clothes,* was all that rang in her head, and the thought made Kate immeasurably sad.

Since the Bees had met during the week and most of them would be going to the party that night at the country club, the Saturday quilting session at Selma's was cancelled for the day. Kate jogged over to Po's and the two sat together at the kitchen table, drinking cups of strong coffee. They sat in silence, absorbing the sadness that was Ann Woods' life, and feeling like they needed to grieve for Laurel St. Pierre a second time.

"Po, it's beginning to make a frightening kind of sense," Kate said, her eyes following a robin as it lighted on a branch, then flew off to its nest.

After leaving school the day before, Kate bought an apple pie at Marla's and took it over to the Hallorans. Ella Halloran's memory was a peculiar thing—some days she barely knew who Kate was, but could tell her what she ate for dinner on her and Danny's wedding day fifty years earlier. Friday was one of those days. She remembered Esther Woods as clear as a Kansas sky.

In starts and stops, Ella told Kate about Ann Woods leaving town. She remembered it, because Esther and that no-good husband of hers up and moved to a bigger house right after the girl left. Seemed so odd, Ella said, that they'd wait until there were only two of them, then move to a big, fancy house. And shortly after that, right after Esther finished sewing a pink brocade suit for Ella to wear to the garden club's spring luncheon, Esther stopped sewing. Didn't need the money, Ella supposed. And not a month or so after that was that car wreck.

"I'm almost sure Picasso never knew about the baby," Po said softly. Kate's news had jarred her. She had built up many scenarios in her mind, but this hadn't been one of them. She knew Laurel had been hurt, she knew she wanted revenge. But the thought of a baby in the middle of it had not occurred to her. "Picasso told me once that Laurel couldn't have children. It was one of the great sadnesses of their life, he said."

"What do you think happened to the baby? I wonder if the father raised it?"

Though she had no reason to conjecture, Po didn't think that was the case. More likely the boy who got her pregnant was the one on the phone that night, telling Ann to get lost, get out of his life. They were just kids. The pieces were slowly coming together and Po almost wished she could stop it. It was a giant ball rolling down the hill, and Po was afraid of what would happen when it crashed at the bottom and all the secrets fell out. "Kate," she asked suddenly, lifting her head as an idea made its way into her head, "did Ella Halloran ever mention where Al Woods worked?"

"She mentioned that he did construction work. It irritated Ella terribly—as if it were any of her business. But she said he'd come into the house while she was there for fittings and he wouldn't have showered. He tracked mud all over the small house and smelled awful, she said. And then he'd sit at the kitchen table and drink beer in his soiled t-shirt. Made her sick, she said."

Po stood and walked over to a small mirror in

the kitchen. She ran a brush through her hair, then slid a light lipstick across her lips and swept blush across her cheekbones, avoiding the woman looking back at her from the mirror, that wise part of her soul who would have told her to mind her own business.

"Kate," she said abruptly, turning away from the mirror and grabbing a jeans jacket from the back of her chair, "Let me give you a ride home. I know you have things to do to get ready for the party and I've a slew of errands to run. Find something lovely to wear tonight, and how about if you and P.J. pick me up at 8?"

Po's trip to the library was brief. Ten minutes with the newspaper obituary records told her all she needed to know about Esther and Al Woods' tragic accident and the funeral. There was one child, the obit read, who now lived on the East Coast. Her name was not mentioned. The newspaper article relating the accident was a little more detailed, and chatty, as small town journalism sometimes is. It told how Al and Esther had attended a company picnic that afternoon, and Al had consumed a tremendous quantity of beer. His blood alcohol level, the article said, was four times the accepted limit. At the time of the accident, they were driving back to a large home that had recently been purchased on a hill just outside town. There was a question about the brakes on Al Woods' new truck, but the weaving that had been viewed by several witnesses made that less important than the fact that Al was very drunk. And, Po thought, there was no family to force an investigation, so it was probably not even attended to. The funeral was private, the article read, as the couple had wished, and the bodies would be cremated. United Quarry had set up a memorial fund with the proceeds to go to Mothers Against Drunk Drivers.

Generous company, Po thought. When Sam died, the college had set up a scholarship fund in his name, and Po was touched by the gesture and knew it would have been just what he wanted. Each year a deserving student was able to attend Canterbury College—and Sam was thought of and honored as the generous, lovely man he was. The memorial fund for Al was another matter. But if it benefited a good cause, Po was for it. On a whim, she typed the words UNITED QUARRY into her search engine, and in an instant, the screen listed pages of newspaper articles detailing the successful company that had its beginnings in Crestwood and now did business in Florida as well. On the home page, Po read about the company's magnanimous giving to charities and political campaigns. She clicked on the ABOUT US button and scanned the names listed on the page—the board of directors and founders and staff—looking for familiar names. Max

Elliott was there, which was no surprise to her. Max was everywhere, a silent, respectable member of more boards and charities than Po could count. Po read on, and then stopped suddenly, her eyes settling on another familiar name.

"Of course," she said out loud. "I should have remembered that." She stopped reading the screen, and looked off into the events of the past few weeks, her heart pounding in her chest. Sam had delighted in her overactive imagination. A necessary tool for a writer, he had said. And maybe that's exactly what she was doing now. Or were the jagged pieces of this puzzle starting to fit together in a way Po couldn't have imagine just a short time ago?

She picked her purse up from the floor and walked slowly out of the library, thinking sadly about Ann Woods, and how her life might have been different.

CHAPTER 26

Po took a deep pink beaded sweater out of her closet and pulled it over her head, then stepped into a long black skirt and fastened it in the back. But clothes for a fancy event were the farthest thing from her mind. Thoughts of Picasso ran through her head—and of all the people who had rallied around them. She dug through her jewelry box and pulled out a chunky rose quartz necklace—a gift from Sam. One of those no-special-day gifts that he sometimes surprised her with. *Why are you on my mind so much today, Sam,* she wondered, looking up, as if Sam Paltrow would suddenly materialize and she could talk all this over with him, listen to his wise words. And, as he always said, ignore them . . . or not. She had no proof for her suspicions, just a bunch of isolated facts that seemed to converge uncomfortably on the same bumpy road.

Po looked in the mirror and fastened the necklace around her neck. She'd see Max tonight. Maybe he could help.

The sound of P.J.'s car in the drive pushed the thoughts into a corner of her mind and she forced a smile in place. This was a special night. Picasso needed them all there as he gave his quilt away to a good cause. Po lifted a soft black shawl from the back of her bedroom chair and hurried downstairs to her waiting ride.

The Crestwood Country Club was south of town, built along the grassy banks of the Emerald River. A golf course wrapped around the property and touched close to the water in places, making it a challenging and energizing course. And down the carefully manicured drive from the main clubhouse, stables housed championship steeds, riding horses, and several show horses owned by members.

Po, P.J., and Kate drove up the long drive to the clubhouse. It was lit all along the way with low gaslights flickering against the dark night.

The drive to the club had been a quiet one. Po sat in the back, alone with her thoughts. But she noticed the pensive look on both Kate and P.J.'s faces, and she wondered briefly if they were all, perhaps, thinking the same thoughts, each in their own way. Thoughts that would eventually emerge, see the light of day, and become real. There was something safe about keeping them inside your head. Just like writing a book, she thought, they could still be manipulated and changed.

But sadly, life wasn't so neat or easily edited.

Po looked up at the well-lit clubhouse. It sparkled with life and gaiety. Tonight would be happy. Tonight they would put aside the worries and suspicions and uncomfortable thoughts and be there for Picasso. Tomorrow would come soon enough.

"Kate," Po said aloud, "you look especially beautiful tonight."

"I second that," P.J. said, looking over at her.

"It's the company," Kate said. "How could someone not feel special with one of you on either side of me?" She tucked an arm in each of theirs as they walked toward the clubhouse. Kate's long deep-blue dress was simple and elegant, *very Kate,* as Po told her. Tiny straps held up the simple silk dress that flowed like liquid silver over Kate's slender hips, down to her ankles, showing off strappy sandals with heels that lifted Kate to nearly P.J.'s height. Her hair was pulled into a knot in the back, fastened with a band and a single daisy.

"My wonder woman," P.J. said, looking into her eyes.

"One who makes you wonder?" was Kate's playful retort.

And she did just that, P.J. thought. Made him wonder about all sorts of things. Good things, tantalizing things. But today she made him wonder how he could keep her safe.

Phoebe and Jimmy Mellon were at the door waiting for them when the threesome walked beneath the canopy and up the wide fan of steps.

"This is the happiest day of my life," Phoebe declared, hugging them. "I get to sit with my best friends at this club that I usually dread going to more than my annual ob-gyn checkup." She hugged Kate and Po, then gave P.J. a kiss on the cheek.

"One glass of wine and all Phoebe's filters disappear," Jimmy said, laughing as she hugged him, too. "Come on in, folks. I echo Phoebe's sentiment, except for that bit about the ob-gyn."

Inside, all was light and airy, and a festive mood drew the crowd through the wide hallways and into the rooms in the back. French doors

212

opened to the terrace, and people spilled outside to look at the moon and enjoy the warm spring air. Waiters and waitresses, carrying trays of wine and champagne, tiny stuffed mushrooms and plump oysters with lemon, wove in and out between happy groups of people.

"Your mother-in-law puts on a fancy party, Phoebs," P.J. observed.

"I know. Can you imagine when the twins turn sixteen?" Phoebe's laughter circled the room and in minutes Eleanor, Maggie, Leah, and her husband Tim found the small group. "Phoebe's laugh is better than a whistle," Leah said. "We just followed the ripples."

"Are Selma and Susan coming?" Po asked.

"They're sitting with the Elderberry merchants, but will join us later," Leah said.

A waiter appeared and passed out tall champagne flutes. "Where is the quilt?" Eleanor asked. "The piece de resistance?"

"Just follow me, folks." Phoebe spun around on her three-inch heels and led them through the crowd and an archway to the room beyond. There on the wall, with tiny lights reflecting off the gold thread that outlined Esther Woods' bird, was Picasso's donation to the evening.

"It looks even more beautiful than I remembered," Kate said softly.

Po stood in front of it, staring up at the amazing design, the flowing curves quilted in pale yellows and golds. And the magnificent bird in the center. It looked so free, she thought, and wondered briefly if Esther's daughter was finally free as well. Po's eyes took in every detail, the border of deep gold fabric, quilted in swirls that mirrored the wings of the bird. Laurel had cared for the quilt like a child, Picasso had said. Mending torn threads, dusting it. Po looked at the border on the bottom and imagined Laurel mending it carefully. A labor of love, she thought. Perhaps to be closer to her mother, Po thought, because the quilt looked to be in excellent condition, without frays or loose threads. But maybe just touching it brought back the few good memories Laurel had when she was Ann Woods.

"It is beautiful, non?"

Po turned around and looked into the pensive face of Picasso. "It is beautiful." Po hugged him and together they looked up at the quilt as if they were standing in the Louvre, looking up at the Mona Lisa.

"I think this is a kind, generous thing you are doing," Po said.

Before Picasso could respond, Bill McKay came up beside them.

"Picasso," Bill said, resting a hand on his shoulder. "What a generous gift."

Po stepped back. Bill was dressed in a fine Italian black suit, looking every bit the wealthy real estate magnate and future politician. His shoulders were broad like a quarterback's, his stance confident and tall.

"You like it, Bill?" Picasso asked.

"It's a wonderful gift. And I for one will make sure it brings in a pretty penny for the SafeHome we're building."

"The auction will be soon?"

"Janna tells me it's after the buffet. After everyone has had a couple glasses of wine." He smiled at Picasso. "That's when everyone gets generous."

The buffet was a glorious affair, and Po almost forgot the heaviness in her heart. After dinner, a dessert bar drew folks back to their feet and they mingled with plates of chocolate-covered strawberries and crème brûlée in their hands, while a harpist played in the background and waiters cleared the tables, preparing for the auction. A dozen or so other gifts—vacations in Colorado, gold chandelier earrings, paintings, memberships to a health club—would be auctioned first, and then Picasso's quilt.

"You could almost forget we're living under this pall of murder, couldn't you?" Maggie said.

Po nodded. "It's good to see Picasso smile. If not for that, I don't think I could have come."

Kate joined them, balancing three glasses of wine in her hands, and they walked onto the terrace together, away from the crowd surrounding

Picasso's quilt. In the distance, they could hear the river moving in the black night. "Laurel's body was found just a little south of here," Maggie said.

Kate nodded. "I wonder when we'll look at the river and not think of her, floating all the way from the bridge."

Po put her hands on the stone railing, looking out into the darkness, half-listening to the conversation. She took a sip of wine, and then put it back down, her mind turning back to Kate's comment. "Kate," she said abruptly, "what did you say?"

"I said the river makes us think of Laurel."

"No, about where she was thrown in the river." Po's heart skipped a beat.

"Oh, just that the spot is near the bridge where the incline is filled with brambles, and it's so far from where she was found. I remember you and mom never wanted us to play over there. It was secluded, kind of scary. It must be a couple miles from where she was found, don't you think?"

"How did you know where she was thrown into the river? Did P.J. tell you?"

"Did I tell her what?" P.J. walked up behind them.

"I wondered how Kate knew where Laurel was thrown into the river." Po tried to keep her voice steady, but the events of the last few days were crowding down on her, squeezing the air out of her lungs.

216

P.J. frowned. "No. I didn't tell Kate that. That information hasn't been released."

Kate looked from Po to P.J. She frowned. "But someone told me where she was thrown in the river."

"Who told you, Kate?" Po asked. Her body tensed.

Kate set her wine glass on the terrace wall. She racked her brain. It shouldn't be difficult to remember—she didn't talk to many people about this. Finally she shook her head. "Sorry, Po, I can't remember. But give me time."

"It might be important, Kate," P.J. said.

"I think it *is* important, P.J.," Po said quietly. "You and I need to have a talk."

The tinkle of a bell announced the beginning of the auction and slowly the crowd began gathering in the auction salon, coffee cups and wine glasses in hand. P.J. looked over at Po as they started inside. He lifted his brows.

"It can wait, P.J.," she said over the crowd. *But not for long,* she thought.

Janna and Bill stood in front of the room with Meredith Mellon, quieting the crowd and announcing the beginning of the auction. The roomful of people clapped hard in appreciation for the work of the chair people, and the auctioneer climbed up to a podium to begin the show.

Po stood in the back, looking across the crowd. Max Elliott caught her eye, and he lifted a hand in a wave, then wove his way to her side. "Po," he whispered. "There's something I want to talk to you about."

Po nodded, and they walked back to the terrace door. "We can see when the quilt auction begins from here," she whispered, then turned her back to the room and looked at Max. "There's something I want to talk to you about, too. Max, you're on the board of United Quarry."

He nodded. "You're a step ahead, as always. I've toyed with breaching client confidentiality, but I ran into Kate today and she told me you were looking up old newspaper articles at the library. I knew you'd come across it."

"Did you know the Woodses, Max?"

Max paused for a long time, and Po wasn't sure he was going to answer her. But it didn't matter now. She knew the answer.

"I knew them in a way," Max said finally. "Al worked for United Quarry. And the company helped him out when he had some personal problems and I handled the checks."

"Helped him out how?"

"Gave them money. I didn't know what it was for. That wasn't my job. But he had problems, and for some reason, United Quarry was helping him out."

"So they gave extra money to Al Woods? Why?"

Max shrugged. "I didn't know then. Or maybe I

didn't want to know. I sent money where I was told to send it. For a long time I sent it to a place in New York, to a relative, to pay for things."

"Ann's aunt."

Max nodded. "I suppose. One of my board functions was to handle special funds, and that's where the money came from."

"Generous company," Po said.

Max heard the sharp edge to Po's voice. He nodded. "More than that. Al got a big raise and a bonus so he could buy that big house. It was odd, made lots of people mad as hell. Al Woods was a drunken bum, and he was treated like a king. No one really mourned when his truck ran off the road that night. No one cared. The company buried them in fine manner and that was that, the end of a chapter."

"Except for a teenage daughter left in New York."

"Right. But she was better off, Po. You didn't know the dad. He was a real mess. But I had trouble with the use of those discretionary funds, the movement of money between the companies owned by the same group, lots of things. So I quit the board and moved on. And I swear I didn't know until recent days what the connection was. But I sure as hell now know why Laurel St. Pierre hated me. She got those checks, saw my name. I was responsible—"

A movement from inside caught their attention

and the lights dimmed briefly, announcing the auction of Picasso's quilt.

"We need to be in there for this," Po said. "But Max, I think I know why Laurel St. Pierre was murdered."

Max stared at her, but before he could pursue her statement, Po had disappeared inside the room. She stood in the back row, watching the hands begin to rise as the auctioneer announced the minimum bid. Max stood in the shadows near the terrace, watching her.

"I have $800," the auctioneer called out in his unique staccato beat.

The room was packed, and all eyes were on the auctioneer as two men stood slightly in front of him, noting the raised hands.

Po heard a familiar voice in front. Bill McKay was bidding on the quilt, keeping his promise to Picasso to raise the ante. Po could see him near the front, Janna pressed closely into his side. They were smiling broadly and Po noticed several flash bulbs go off.

Another bid came from the right, and a hand answered from a few rows behind. Po stared at the quilt, still lit with the tiny lights, showing the amazing craftsmanship of a woman who had so little in her life.

Again, the bid was countered, and Po watched in fascination as it bounced back and forth between an art dealer in the back of the room, and a stranger up in the front. Po didn't recognize him, but Max whispered that he was with United Quarry, a board member that had been there when Max was on the board. Po stared at the man, and watched as the gallery owner responded. Po strained to see if the man in the front was bidding on his own. A turn of the man's gray head, a nod in the direction of the audience, was all Po needed to see.

The click in Po's head was so loud she was sure the whole room must have heard it. The care Laurel had given to the quilt. The break-in at Picasso's lovely home, looking for something, something Laurel had left behind. The few missing pieces to the puzzle.

And without a second thought, Po stepped forward, out of the shadows, and in a loud clear voice, joined the bidding.

Several heads turned to hear who had challenged the two men, but the gallery owner immediately answered Po's bid, and heads quickly turned back to the auctioneer. A rush of excitement ran through the crowd as they felt the thrill of the chase. When the man from United Quarry countered the bid, Po had had enough. She needed to stop this. The bidding was up to three thousand dollars. Po took a deep breath. *Sorry, Sam,* she murmured. *I know you don't like frivolous spending, but it's for a very good cause, believe me.*

Po cleared her throat, and in a loud voice, bid $10,000 on Esther Woods' bird quilt.

A chain of oohs and aahs passed through the crowd like the wave at a baseball game. Then a lone individual started clapping, and in seconds the entire room burst into a noisy show of appreciation for Po's generous gift. To outbid her, should anyone be so inclined, would be an embarrassment. And the gesture would draw unfortunate attention to the bidder. Po smiled and ignored the frantic beating of her heart. She'd won.

CHAPTER 27

Bill McKay, with Janna at his side, concluded the auction with a gracious thanks to Picasso St. Pierre for the gift of his quilt, and an equal thanks to the winner of the evening's auction, Mrs. Portia Paltrow.

The crowd loved it all, the competition, the cause, the food and the wine and the invitation to move into the other room where there'd be dancing and music.

"Po!" Kate said, weaving her way through the crowd to Po's side. "I can't believe it. You have Laurel's quilt. I had no idea you were going to do this."

Po smiled, but she could hardly find her voice. And she surely couldn't admit that she had no earthly intention of spending $10,000 on a quilt when she walked through the door three hours ago. She took a deep breath to ward off the wave of weariness that pressed down on her. Max brought her a glass of water and she nodded in gratitude. She drained the glass.

"Po, are you all right?" Kate asked, noticing Po's demeanor.

"I'm fine, honey," Po said. "Tired, is all. I've never won an auction before."

"Would you like us to take you home?"

"No, go dance. You've got to dance with the one who brung you, didn't you know?"

"Of course I know. You and mom used to recite that silly ditty to me before every dance I ever went to."

"Well, then let's do it," P.J. said, cupping her elbow in the palm of his hand. "Po, you sit, we'll dance. Max, you keep an eye on Po. I don't trust her these days." He nodded at Max, then swept Kate onto the dance floor and out of their sight.

As Kate and P.J. made their way to the dance floor, Bill walked up, his arm outstretched to shake Po's hand. "Congratulations, m'lady. You've got yourself a magnificent quilt, and the SafeHome fund has a generous contribution."

"Thank you, Billy," Po said.

"You look a little tired. Max? Want to give a generous lady a ride home?"

"I'm not ready just yet, Billy, I'd like to collect

my quilt first. I believe the ladies are taking it down."

"It may take awhile, Po. I hear it took them all afternoon to put it up after Picasso dropped it off. I'll have a couple of the fellows help me fold and wrap it, and I'll drop it off myself tomorrow."

Meredith Mellon squeezed her beaded body in front of Bill and gave Po a hug. "You are wonderful, Po," she said. "What a nice gift." She turned toward Bill. "And as for you, sir, you are wanted in the lobby. There's a photographer waiting to take a picture of you and Janna for Kansas City's *Independent*." Bill looked at Po, then glanced over toward the lobby where the photographer stood over his pile of equipment. Janna stood next to him, waiting for Bill. "Po, you'll be okay?" he asked.

"Come, Bill. This is important for your campaign," Meredith instructed, and she took him by the arm, leading him away.

"Max," Po said abruptly. "Would you please take me home?"

It took Max and Leah's husband, Tim Sarandon, to get the quilt folded and placed in the back of Max's Pathfinder, but within ten minutes, Po and Max were climbing into the car and bringing the engine to life.

"Did you tell Kate you were leaving, Po? Won't she worry?"

Po frowned. She should have told Kate before

she went onto the dance floor. But she'd let Phoebe know, so the word would pass to Kate and she would know Po was fine. It was a good moment to sneak out without causing commotion, and Po didn't want to draw attention to herself. She just wanted to be home. She wanted to be home with her quilt. She needed to know she was right before she called in the police and ruined a person's life.

Kate stood on the side porch of the club, watching Max's car race off into the night. She'd left P.J. alone on the dance floor, rushing to find Po. She had finally remembered. She knew who told her where Laurel St. Pierre was thrown into the Emerald River—and she needed to tell Po.

Po and Max drove down the curving drive, passed the railed fields where the horses grazed, and headed home. They drove in silence for several miles, crossing over the bridge, where it all began, then past the sleeping Elderberry neighborhood.

"He was bidding for someone else," Max finally said. Although he spoke the words, they were pulled from Po's thoughts.

Po nodded. "I could see the exchange, but only because I was looking for it."

"I should have seen everything, Po. Should have seen it years ago. The company was playing God, manipulating people's lives."

"It wasn't the company," Po said. "It was the man at the top. He held the strings, Max. People did what he wanted."

Max turned into Po's driveway and pulled the car up to the back door. Without a word they got out of the car, opened the back of Max's SUV, and gently removed their precious cargo. Around them the night was still and black, the warm spring air and sweet smell of the lilac bushes masking the dread in Po's heart.

Po held the door open for Max, then switched on lights as Max carried the quilt over to the kitchen table.

"Max, I didn't mean to involve you in this—"

"Po, I became involved when I sent money to Ann Woods' aunt in New York. I didn't realize until we put pieces together today that it was probably used for hospital bills for Ann, or whatever they arranged for her and the baby. But it doesn't matter. I was involved when the money from the foundation was used to buy Al Woods a house. It didn't make sense to a lot of us, but no one talked about it. No one knew, or if they did, they didn't say, that it was to cover up the family's sins. But we didn't know because we didn't ask or look or try to put it all together."

Po waved Max's words away and walked over to the quilt. "Max, it's done. The important thing now is to prove it and not let any more lives be torn apart in the process. And I think Laurel's quilt holds the answer. Picasso told me this was Laurel's child, the one she could never have. *Her life,* he said. I think Picasso meant those words far more literally than he even knew. Laurel was blackmailing people, or at the least, holding information that would ruin their lives. Max, if I'm right, this quilt is the key to Laurel's life—and to her death."

Gently, as if rubbing a baby's back, Po padded the quilt around the edges. Esther had used a thick batting for the interlining and Po couldn't feel any bumps in it. Her heart was tight in her chest. Somehow she knew the quilt had to be the answer. Or a murderer would go free. She lifted the edge of the quilt and looked at the double binding Esther had used to finish the edges, making them strong, less likely to tear or come apart. And then Po saw it. The careful disruption of the quilting pattern, the new threads that held the binding on. The fabric was slightly darker along a portion of the edge, probably oil from Laurel's hands as she sat with the quilt, pulling it apart, and burying her life inside of it.

Po took a scissors from the kitchen drawer and began snipping the new stitches Laurel had applied to the backing. She must have done this many times, Po thought. Carefully, she smoothed the binding flat against the table, sliding her fingers beneath the double layer of batting. Her fingers slipped in easily and immediately touched up against stiff paper. Slowly Po pulled out an envelope buried between the layers of fill. She reached in again, and found three more pieces of paper hidden in Laurel's quilt.

Max watched in silence as Po pulled the envelopes from the quilt. "How did you know, Po?"

"It was Picasso. He told me Laurel used to take the quilt down all the time to repair it and dust it. When I looked at it more closely, I realized it wouldn't have needed that kind of repair. Esther was a master seamstress and quilter. She used double binding on this quilt and strong quilting thread. Hanging on a wall wouldn't cause it to fall apart. Laurel was doing something else with it.

"And then there was the break-in at Picasso's. Why would anyone break into his house and not take some of the lovely things Laurel had purchased? He or she was looking for something, and they didn't find it. There had to be something there that Laurel had hidden and someone wanted. What better place to hide the secrets of her life than in her mother's quilt?"

The envelopes weren't sealed, and Po pulled a yellowed photograph out of the first one. She held it up to the light and recognized Esther Woods. She was sitting on a couch with her arms wrapped around a little girl at her side. It was Laurel and her mother, in maybe one of the few peaceful moments of their lives. The second envelope was bigger and held a check for $50,000 made out to Ann Woods from United Quarry and never cashed.

Beside her, Max recognized his own signature and stiffened. "Now I know why she hated me so. She knew all along I was somehow involved in sending the money."

Her payoff, Po thought. Have your baby and stay out of our lives. And he'd made sure she couldn't come back home—Al Woods wouldn't allow it now. The last envelope had legal papers —a medical report, and a birth certificate and death certificate, all in one package. It was for Ann's baby, born too early and with too much trauma to make it in life. And a medical record detailing the damage to her body that would prevent more pregnancies. Po put on her glasses and read the fine print on the birth certificate. Ann Woods was listed as the mother, and, as Po had suspected, probably for days now, Bill McKay was the father. The high school football player—captain of the idolized Hatchets, with whom Ann had fallen in love. And who on a dare, perhaps, got her pregnant and then threw her away.

"I never thought of looking in the quilt for the records until Picasso told me about it the other night in the restaurant, and told me how she treated it. You're smarter than I am, Po."

Po and Max spun around and stared at Bill McKay.

He'd come in the front door, still elegant in his Italian suit, and stood just inside the dark hallway, staring at the two figures standing over the quilt. Near him, one step in front, was Kate.

Po's breath caught in her throat. Her eyes were riveted to the gun pressed tightly into Kate's back.

"Bill . . ." Po began. She took a step toward Kate, her arms reaching out to her.

"Back up," Bill said.

His voice was eerily calm. They could have been talking about his campaign, or P.J. scoring a touchdown.

Bill looked sideways at Kate. "Pretty Kate should have minded her own business. I found her out in front, headed for your back door."

Bill moved closer to the table, pushing Kate along with him and urging Max and Po to step back. He stared down at the photograph and papers spread across the top of the quilt. The birth certificate was in the center and his name popped up off the bottom of the page. Bill turned white.

"What a fool she was," he said. "It was all a joke, you know. The football team dared me. They do it every year. Quarterback dare. But she wasn't supposed to get pregnant. Then she wanted me to marry her!" A laugh followed, and he shook his head and looked at Max and Po, as if they would shake their head and *tsk* at Ann Woods' foolishness. And then he added quietly, "I didn't even know her name. I thought it was Carrie."

Beside him Kate's blood churned and her face turned bright red with anger. Watching her from across the room, Po felt her anger and prayed she wouldn't do anything foolish.

"That's why you'd never eat at Picasso's," Po said calmly, trying to lessen the electricity in the room.

Bill nodded. "I knew she was here—she called me once and told me who she was, that she'd lost the kid. Then she told me she thought the whole town would be interested in the story, and she had all the pieces she needed to make it believable."

"And this wasn't as easy to clean up as when your father neatly sent Ann away and paid off Al Woods," Po said. Po suspected strongly that the drunken accident that took Ann's parents to their death was far more than that. Brakes had probably been tampered with, and Al and Esther died in a very convenient accident. It would never be proven now, but the tragedy of Laurel's death could be.

"I knew your father owned several companies," Po continued, always keeping Kate in the corner of her eye, as if seeing her there would keep her safe. Talking to Bill seemed to calm him some, so Po continued, her heart wedged painfully in her chest. "But it wasn't until I read the accounts of

231

the accident, then probed a little deeper into United Quarry, that I realized Jackson McKay was the CEO."

"My dad was a genius at keeping things in separate compartments, even me. But he was never mayor." Bill thought he heard a noise and glanced toward the back door, then back to Po and Max. He nodded toward the door. "My car is down the street. It's good you're both here. Maybe once you're gone, this can end. It would have all been okay, you know, if she hadn't come back. Couldn't leave it alone. She was going to package it all up, then send it all to the paper. Foolish, horrible twit." He looked at Po calmly and for a minute they could have been talking about the weather. "My father's not the only one who can plan, you see. It's all set up for me now. Janna's father will invest in my ventures. I'll be a successful businessman. Then mayor—they like me, you know, all these people. Even Picasso likes me. My life will be bigger than Jackson T. McKay ever dreamed of."

The bitterness in his voice startled Po for a minute. "Billy, I don't think you want to harm more people. This doesn't help you get back at your dad. Maybe you didn't even mean to harm Laurel."

Kate moved slightly and Bill took her arm, pinching it tightly. He looked back at Po. "I thought I could talk to her. But she didn't want to talk—she wanted to ruin me, and she wouldn't back down. She wouldn't listen . . ." His voice trailed off as if his mind was going in different directions at once. The carefully held together Bill McKay was unraveling.

"Janna—she's a bright girl, if a little drab. And her family situation more than makes up for that. But she's like all women—too nosey and manipulating—and she almost ruined it. She thought I was meeting a woman that night and she was jealous. So she followed me and hid in the bushes. She knew it all. Knew the wine guy was blackmailing me. Knew how Laurel died—"

"And where," Kate said. "Janna was the one who mentioned where Laurel was killed, Po. I finally remembered."

"And the bleach on the quilt, that was Janna, wasn't it?" Po asked. "She couldn't bear the thought of losing you to prison. She wanted to protect you."

Bill shook his head at the memory. "That fat woman in the bakery told me about the bleach, and I knew immediately from the look on Janna's face that she had done it. I was furious. She could have ruined everything."

Kate's brows pulled together when Billy pushed the metal more forcefully into her shoulder blades, but she kept talking. "Janna hung around us enough to know that we were getting closer. And she would have given her life to protect the only man who had ever paid any attention to her."

"She's as bad as the rest of them. Doesn't think logically."

"She loves you, Billy. And now you're ruining her life, too," Kate said.

"Stop—all of you. Let me think." He rubbed his temples and looked around the room, like a kid looking for a place to hide. Then he backed up toward the door, his gun still pressed into Kate's side.

"We'll go to the quarry," he said at last. "That's where I met Jason Sands that night." He laughed lightly. "Now why did Laurel confide in that useless guy? She wasn't very good at picking her men, was she? Come, friends, let's go."

"I don't think so, Billy." And before Bill could register that the voice was directly behind him, P.J. knocked the gun to the floor, twisted Billy's arm in a painful grip, and shoved him into the hands of half the Crestwood police force, waiting with open arms on the front steps.

"Po, you've got to start locking your doors," P.J. muttered, and then he filled his arms with the woman who had disappeared from the dance floor an hour before, and never returned. "You're supposed to dance with the one who brung you," he whispered into her neck. "Not run off with the quarterback."

Po watched the two of them as she wiped the tears from her eyes, her heart still pounding as the sirens and cars started up and tore down the street. *Oh, Liz,* Po moaned softly. *That was surely a close one.*

EPILOGUE

It was bouillabaisse, of course, that was featured at the unveiling of Picasso's quilt. And a fine arugula salad, with greens from the new organic farm that Picasso had discovered just south of town. He'd baked the baguettes that morning, and whipped up bowls of butter with snips of rosemary tossed in for color and flavor. The restaurant was closed to the public for the evening, and only special friends and Elderberry merchants filled the small restaurant.

A warm breeze filled the restaurant with the smells of May—lilac and tulips, violets and pansies. Beside the restaurant, flowering crab apple trees and pink dogwoods, lit from beneath with tiny lights, welcomed the guests.

All of the Queen Bees were there, having worked feverishly all month to finish the quilt. Max Elliott came, and the whole street of Elderberry merchants and spouses. Ambrose and Jesse provided the champagne, and Andy Haynes played his guitar in the background. When Picasso pulled the sheet down and revealed the

French Quarter quilt, its boiling pot a shiny blue-black image at the bottom, and the brilliant, colorful fish soaring across the pieced background, there wasn't a dry eye in the room.

"It is perfect," Picasso declared, lifting his glass of champagne. "And you are friends like none other."

The toasts echoed around the room, cheers and hoots and sighs of relief.

Janna Hathaway had disappeared from town, scooped up by another domineering father. Selma wasn't going to press charges for the damaged quilt—it was such a minor thing, done out of fear for a man not worthy of her love. And Janna had suffered tremendously in the process.

Billy had felt nothing for Janna, the Bees had conjectured. She was a stepping-stone for him. And that was just another sad, cruel piece of the whole horrible story.

"Po, what will you do with your quilt?" Picasso asked as the happy crowd milled around them.

"A perfect solution, Picasso. The one good thing to come out of all of this is SafeHome. They made a hunk of money at the gala, and donations are still coming in, so it will become a reality. Meredith Mellon has taken over the whole project, so you know it will happen. I suggested she call it Laurel's Place—and the quilt will hang in the entry."

Picasso leaned over and kissed her on the

cheek. Tears glistened in his eyes, but his face was full of happiness.

Waiters appeared then, as if by magic, carrying colorful bowls heaped full of steaming bouillabaisse, and people moved toward the white-clothed tables.

"Where's Kate?" Po asked as Max took her elbow and directed her to a table by the window. Po knew that Kate had had nightmares following Bill McKay's arrest, and she was filled with an anger that Po knew would take her awhile to shake. But as Kate would do, she was purging it in an appropriate way—using her summer photography class to focus on images of strong women, taking charge of their lives. They'd have a show at the end of summer, and sell the framed photos to benefit Laurel's Place. P.J. had found it difficult to be apart from Kate for more than a few minutes at a time after the events of the past weeks. And Po knew that she would no longer be the only one looking out for her best friend's daughter.

"I saw her near the kitchen door earlier," Phoebe said, as she scooped Emma up in her arms. Jimmy followed close behind with little Jude toddling beside him.

Po smiled at the twins, then moved around the room, searching for the bright red blouse Kate had worn that night. As she wove her way through the crowd toward the back of the restaurant, a flash of red through a rear window caught her eye. Po walked over to the back door and looked out into the dark night. "Kate?" she said softly.

There was no answer, and Po stood there for a minute, her eyes adjusting to the darkness. And then a sound drew her eyes to the flowering crab that Picasso had planted out in the alley. *A touch of beauty,* he called it.

And that it was, Po thought, as she saw the two figures beneath its branches. She stood there for just a brief moment, watching P.J. and Kate. They were wrapped in one another's arms, shadowed from moonlight by the branches of the tree. The nightmares had stopped for Kate, Po thought, and she nodded at the sight that filled her heart to overflowing.

I told you it would be okay, Liz, she whispered to her best friend. *Have I ever let you down?* And with a lighter step, Po and joined her friends over a heaping bowl of bouillabaisse, some laughter, and bonds of friendship that lit the small restaurant from within.

Center Point Publishing
600 Brooks Road • PO Box 1
Thorndike ME 04986-0001 USA

(207) 568-3717

US & Canada:
1 800 929-9108
www.centerpointlargeprint.com